the lipstick laws

Written by Amy Holder

GRAPHIA

Houghton Mifflin Harcourt
Boston   New York   2011

To Boom Boom, whom I love and miss.

Copyright © 2011 by Amy Holder

All rights reserved. Published in the United States by Graphia,
an imprint of Houghton Mifflin Harcourt Publishing Company.

For information about permission to reproduce selections from this book,
write to Permissions, Houghton Mifflin Harcourt Publishing Company,
215 Park Avenue South, New York, New York 10003.

Graphia and the Graphia logo are registered trademarks of
Houghton Mifflin Harcourt Publishing Company.

www.hmhbooks.com

The text of this book is set in Adobe Garamond Pro.

Library of Congress Cataloging-in-Publication Data
Holder, Amy.
The Lipstick Laws / Amy Holder.
p. cm.
Summary: When Britney, the most popular girl at Penford High School,
invites April Bowers to her lunch table April is thrilled with her sudden change
in status, but soon finds that Britney's friendship comes at a steep price.
ISBN 978-0-547-36306-6
[1. Popularity—Fiction. 2. Conformity—Fiction. 3. Body image—Fiction.
4. Self-esteem—Fiction. 5. High schools—Fiction. 6. Schools—Fiction.] I. Title.
PZ7.H702Lip 2011
[Fic]—dc22
2010027416

Manufactured in the United States of America
DOM 10 9 8 7 6 5 4 3 2 1
4500285047

chapter one

Sitting near Darci Madison on the school bus is enough to put anyone with woman-sprout issues over the edge. Sure, she might wear a push-up bra, but the point is that she has more than enough there to push up. I, on the other hand, don't. I glance down to critique my Kleenex sculpture . . . and can't help but compare her jiggle to my stationary tissue wads.

Tormented by the abundant boobage sitting across from me, I hesitatingly admit to myself that yes, I am an addict. I'm not a drug addict—no, too risky and expensive. I'm not a sex addict—please, I haven't even had a decent make-out session sans drool and cheap cologne. Something that others blow their noses into happens to be my addiction of choice. I, April Bowers, am a tissue-wasting, size-34C-obsessed bosom sculptor. Yes, I confess . . . I am a bra stuffer.

As I ponder the injustice of having a bellybutton that sticks out farther than my 34AA chest, I begin to wonder if instead of growing out, my boobage is growing inward. Maybe if I were inside out I'd have the body of a goddess.

What a fantastic theory.

My brief smile is abruptly halted by a speed bump that makes Darci's ginormous boobs heave from her chest. A panic bubble lodges in my throat as the bus slows to a stop. The bus driver opens the door with a shrewd grin. She watches me in the rearview mirror as I approach the exit.

"First-day jitters?" she says.

I glance down at my chewed fingernails, smiling passively. First-day jitters doesn't quite describe where I'm at right now. Early-life crisis is more like it.

With heavy feet, I slowly slink down the steps to emerge onto the hazardous war zone that most refer to as Penford High School. The ominous sand-colored building stands before me like a large enemy barrack. Déjà vu hits me at warp speed. It seems like just yesterday I was making the same brutal walk of shame as a brand-new freshman with no friends. This year two things have changed: I'm a sophomore, and I'm not new anymore. But one thing remains the same: I have no friends.

I feel vulnerably alone making my way through the groups of bubbly girls conversing about their summer hookups, vacations, and shopping sprees. This is the moment I've been dreading since Haley Lucas, the one good friend I made last year, moved to Dorothy's wonderland in July.

Delaying the inevitable, I stop to pull out my compact to make sure my war paint is still intact. A wave of relief comes over me. My makeup still looks okay. It's amazing what superficial reassurance can do for someone marching to her social death.

Just as I'm shutting my compact, I notice a reflection that I'm not at all happy to see—Delvin McGerk. Also known as King Stalker McGerk of Loserhood. I walk briskly, hoping to slip into the sea of students unseen by his radar eyes. My hopes are smashed when he catches up to me, waving excitedly. Frustration floods my body as I glance over at him. His creepy eyes look like huge silver dollars lurking behind his thick magnifying glasses.

"April Bowers, you're looking rather illustrious today," he says.

Why does he talk like that? More important, why does he talk to *me?*

"Thanks, Delvin," I mumble, looking to the left to avoid eye contact.

"Guess what?"

"What?" I huff irritably.

Predictably, he grins and croaks, "My mom talked to your mom yesterday."

Bingo. I knew he was gonna say that. After all, it's the only thing we have in common. Yes, we both have moms . . . and yes, they know each other.

"No way, McGerk. I don't believe it." My sarcasm is so thick, I could spoonfeed it to a baby.

"It's true," he insists, adjusting his lopsided glasses.

I stare at his ruler-parted floppy brown hair, wondering what planet he came from.

An uncomfortable silence ensues.

It just so happens that my mom and Delvin's mom are old sorority sisters. Before the move here last year, I had high hopes that Delvin would have movie star looks and a playboy reputation that would skyrocket me to popularity as soon as I stepped foot in the school. Having heard stories about how pretty and popular Patty McGerk was in college, I couldn't help but believe her attractiveness and social skills would be passed down to her only son. My disappointment was monumental when during our first introduction, Delvin spent a half hour explaining aeronautics while obsessively adjusting his lopsided glasses.

Lucky me. Since then, he has convinced himself that our mothers' friendship gives him the right to be a total stalker.

"Sooo . . ." He chuckles, nervously twisting his backpack straps. If I were up for it, he'd spend the whole day exchanging awkward glances.

"Delvin, I've gotta go," I say sharply, leaving no room for mixed signals.

He winks, like he's about to say something über suave. "Well then, I guess I'll see ya later."

I pray he's wrong.

His chapped lips curl into a ridiculously cheesy smile before we part ways. I'm blinded by the sheen of ten pounds of metal securely fastened to his teeth. Why couldn't my mom be old friends with Troy Hoffman's mom? Probably the same reason I have boobs the size of sesame seeds.

I clutch my class schedule tightly and continue my march through the double doors of doom. The hall is bustling with all the personalities one would expect to find in a recipe for teenage stew:

Deliciously Dramatic Teenage Stew

Ingredients:
— Athletic muscle-head beef types
— Tall, gangly carrot types
— Self-conscious round potato types
— Angst-ridden emotional onion types (with too many layers to peel)
— Bully shredded-cabbage types who leave you with stomach cramps and gas

- Shy bouillon cube types who dissolve into obscurity
- Social butterfly bean types—beans, beans, the magical fruit; the more you eat, the more you toot . . . or in this case, talk
- And finally (drumroll, please), stuck-up acidic tomato juice types who cover all the above-mentioned with their gossiping slime

Cooking Directions:

Stir together until uncomfortably blended under the high heat pressure of a social nightmare. Let simmer for nine months out of the year, but please don't over-cook . . . Rumors have the tendency to become vile if cooked too long. Remember to store in an airtight container to ensure drama does not become stale.

In my former life, I was a social butterfly bean type. However, upon transferring schools, I immediately transformed into a shy bouillon cube type. Being comparable to a cube of evaporated meat extract is disheartening to say the least.

After hustling through the strong whiff of simmering personalities, I find my homeroom. I beeline it for the first empty desk I see to sit my socially suffering butt down.

"Pssst—April," an annoying voice calls out from the back of the classroom.

I look back at my older brother. He loves to humiliate me in groups. Sadly for me, homerooms are alphabetized, not separated by grade level. Apparently living with him isn't punishment enough.

"Hi, Aaden." I cringe.

"How was your ride on the yellow honker?" He gestures his scrawny arm like he's honking a horn. "Honk! Honk!"

Obviously he feels totally superior because Jeffrey Higgins drives him to school every day. Don't get me wrong: I'm not jealous that my brother doesn't have to put up with the tortures of the school bus . . . mainly because Jeffrey laughs like a goat. And really, would I want to be stuck in a car every morning with a goat? No, probably not.

"Fabulous," I say listlessly, refusing to indulge my brother's humiliation attempt. With a swift flip of my long curls, I turn to face forward again. I stare at the clock on the front wall counting down the seconds until school is out, while the rest of my homeroom fills with gossip and hearsay.

"Settle down, kids, settle down!"

Holy crapoli! Why is Mr. Stuart in my homeroom? My stomach lunges to my feet at the sight of him. Where is Mrs. Clark? Did he lock her in a janitor's closet? God, please let this be a joke.

"Mrs. Clark is on maternity leave. I'm your new homeroom teacher," he says, looking like a constipated Marine general set on going to the bathroom.

"Another year, fresh faces, and plenty of learning to fill those hungry, young, partially corrupted minds . . ."

Muffled laughter comes from the middle of the group.

"Something funny, Mr. Baker?" his voice booms.

"No, sir. Sorry, sir." The husky jock slouches in his chair.

"Don't let those girly giggles follow you to football practice, or you'll be doing extra sets!" He glowers at the jock.

Mr. Stuart puts the *scar* in *scary*. I find myself staring at the graffiti on my desk that's immortalized teen POWs from years past. I'm pretty sure that eye contact with this beast may result in physical harm.

"As many of you know, I am Mr. Stuart."

By the way, he so does not look like a Mr. Stuart . . . maybe a Mr. Gladiator Man, Mr. Warlord, Mr. Roid Rage, or even a Mr. I Want to Eat Your New Puppy for Lunch . . . but not a Mr. Stuart.

He paces the front of the classroom with his brawny arms crossed against his inflated chest. A large vein bulges from his forehead as he lectures. "I'm a champion on the field and in the classroom. This is *my* show, and if any of you think otherwise, you'll be cast in a little reality show that I like to call detention!"

Mr. Stuart pauses to scan the room for victims.

"If any of you are lucky enough to have me as your history teacher too, well, kudos to you." He claps his enormous hands contemptuously. I marvel at the huge meat hooks, imagining their past casualties. Images of broken bones and ripped flesh twirl around my mind like a carousel.

Mr. Roid Rage sits in a chair at least four sizes too small behind a desk that is comparatively tiny against his massively muscular frame. His right hand engulfs a red pen. Silence gags the room.

"Time for attendance," he grumbles through gritted teeth.

One by one, names are announced and acknowledged by their owners with a "here," "present," or a trembling raised finger. I start sweating the closer he gets to my name.

"Aaden Bowers."

"He-re." My brother's voice quivers with fear.

"April Bowers."

Gulp! Dear Lord, save me. I raise my hand in recognition since my mouth is paralyzed with anxiety.

"Siblings, I presume. Double the Bowerses, double the fun. I'll have to keep an eye on you two." Mr. Stuart cracks his knuckles.

My gosh, this year is going so much worse than I had predicted. So much worse until . . .

"Matthew Brentwood."

Silence.

"Second chance—Matthew Brentwood," Mr. Warlord repeats, looking up from the sheet of names.

A couple seconds later the door swings open and the most gorgeous guy I've ever seen in my life walks in . . . looking rather perplexed, I might add.

"I went to the wrong room." His words are like melted chocolate. His smile is to die for. His model face tops off his perfectly tall, lean, tanned body . . . like frosting on a delectable cupcake. He is *purr-r-r-r-r-fect!*

"Let me guess. Matthew Brentwood?"

Surprised by the nasty tone of Mr. Gladiator Man's voice, he mutters, "Yeah."

"You're late!" Mr. Stuart snaps.

"Sorry. I'm new here." Matthew's sparkling green eyes become tense with worry.

"Well, take a seat already! What do you think, Brentwood, you're on stage or something? This isn't the drama club!"

Matthew hurries to the first seat he finds. His delicious hot-guy aroma overwhelms my nostrils as he speeds past me. I can't help but look back at him. He looks like an Abercrombie model. Sure, after walking into the flames of wrath in homeroom 119, he looks a little like he's just choked on a corkscrew. Nevertheless, he is BEEEE-YOOOOU-TI-FUL!

Mr. Stuart continues taking attendance. However, in my mind, his booming voice slowly drones and morphs into a symphony of sappy love songs. The next ten minutes fly by with thoughts of Matthew grabbing me in a passionate embrace of lust. By the time the bell rings for first period, I've planned steamy make-out sessions, the spring formal, a wedding, children, and the rest of my natural life with Mr. Hottie-Body Brentwood.

Then, reality strikes. I have gym class first period, and I'd rather drill a screw through my big toe.

chapter two

In my opinion, the person who created the torture device called gym class should be clobbered with an enormous frozen cucumber. Not to mention, the person who decided it would be a great idea to schedule me in first period gym every Monday, Wednesday, and Friday also deserves a heavy-handed whacking with the same frozen cucumber.

To avoid the risk of anyone spotting my Kleenex cleavage, I change in the private bathroom next to the main locker area. I truly can't trust any activity that requires me to change out of my normal attire during the school day . . . which boils down to gym class, drama class, and talent shows—all equally shameful in my book.

I sulk into the gymnasium to join the rest of the girls waiting for our gym teacher to make her entrance. Immediately, I spot Britney Taylor instructing five girls on how she lost six and a half pounds on a sugar-free Popsicle diet over the summer.

"It's all about willpower. Some of us just have more than others," she says proudly, holding her chin high. Shallow words continue to dance from her mouth with the superiority that only Britney Taylor exudes. "Remember, a growling stomach is just a round of applause for a job well done."

Hanging on her every word, the girls nod devoutly in agreement. They stare at her like the adoring fans they are. This is nothing new. Everyone treats Britney like she's a princess.

"Great," I mutter under my breath. She's the last person I want to see in my gym class. How can a girl feel confident in gym clothes next to her? Especially when she's wearing those mega short shorts that only an ultra-scandalous pop star would wear while lounging on a tour bus.

Positioning myself on the outskirts of the group of girls, I try to look busy. I dawdle with the seams in my shorts, tie and retie my shoes, look for split ends, and inspect my nail beds . . . all to obscure the fact that I have no one to socialize with.

"Good morning," Ms. Hoopensteiner finally greets us, cradling a basketball. I've never been so relieved to see a gym teacher in my life.

"For those of you who haven't had me before, my name is Ms. Hoopensteiner. But you can call me Ms. Hoops," she says, sounding as if she's sucked in at least a dozen helium balloons for breakfast. "If you can't already tell by my freakishly tall stature"—she snorts, amused by her own joke—"you might be able to gather from my last name that I like to play basketball."

I have doubts that she's tall enough to put a letter in a mailbox, let alone a big orange ball in a ten-foot-high hoop. Despite being tiny, her athletic abilities are impressive.

"In fact," she continues, "I love all balls."

"No way. All futch gym teachers are lezzies," Britney says under her breath, flipping her long blond hair as an exclamation point.

Ms. Hoops ignores the remark, puts the ball down, and clears her throat. "All balls meaning basketballs, soccerballs, footballs, lacrosse balls, tennis balls, bowling balls—heck, even snowballs! In fact, a snowball fight is a great activity to strengthen your hammies, quads, glutes, triceps, and biceps," she says, pointing out the muscles on her pint-size frame.

"Now, girls, time for your gym partners."

Groans flood the gymnasium. She's the only gym teacher in the school who doesn't let students pick their own partner. This worked out to my advantage last year, when I was paired with Haley. I hope my good fortune continues this year.

The squatty teacher begins calling off names. I pray that I don't get paired with Britney or any of her idolizing worshipers. I don't think I can handle the pressure of comparing myself to their perfectness. Unfortunately, I jinx myself.

"April Bowers and Britney Taylor, please pair up and stand with the rest of the line."

Darn it! Haley would die if she knew this was happening to me right now. She hates Britney.

I make my way over to the blond goddess as she whispers "Who?" to a pretty brunette.

"Hi, I'm April," I say politely.

"Oh, hi." Her menacing brown eyes shatter the little confidence I have. "Are you new here or something? I've never seen you."

I pause before I answer. Britney and I were in the same math class last year. In fact, I sat a few seats behind her. Is she so self-absorbed, she's never noticed me? Or worse, am I so uninteresting that I've never been noticed? Feeling like a complete loser already, I can't bring myself to remind her of this.

"Yeah, I'm new."

She stares me up and down appraisingly.

"Welcome to the Roc," she says. *The Roc* is a term that some people living around Rochester, New York, use to make it sound cooler than it really is.

"Thanks," I say, shocked that she's being so welcoming.

Her perfectly sculpted eyebrows furrow in superficial judgment. She nods hastily in acknowledgment and then sneers at Ms. Hoopensteiner's back, blurting, "It's total bunk that we don't get to pick our own partner."

What an endearing comment. Immediately, my self-consciousness skyrockets. I have a sneaking suspicion that Britney has this effect on everyone. She flips her bouncy, long blond locks, just barely smacking me in the face, and turns to join the line of pairs. I follow her scent of expensive shampoo to the wall. I can't help but wonder if the rumor about her having a birthmark in the shape of a Playboy Bunny is true.

After a horrendous fitness test during which I realize that I have the upper-body strength of a soggy green bean, Ms. Hoops releases us to get changed. Being Britney's gym partner means that I'm assigned a gym locker next to hers. The horrifying notion of having to change around her nearly gives me a heart attack. I try to think of every possible way not to change my shirt in front of her. Someone with her kind of body won't be able to sympathize with the torment that's led me to a tissue addiction. Awkwardness creeps up my spine. I can tell she's curious to see if I have any cellulite, ugly moles, or unshaven hair underneath my clothes that she can gossip about later.

"That's a really cute skirt," she says with surprise that I should probably be offended by.

Brilliant! I think this is my chance.

"Thanks. Check out the designs on the back pockets." I'm a genius. I swiftly turn my butt around to face her while simultaneously changing my shirt. Diversion—it works every time.

"Super cute," she says, not even catching on.

I smile at her compliment, hoping she's being sincere. Fashion praise from Britney Taylor is like a Grammy to a new vocal artist.

"Crap," she gripes, fumbling through her makeup bag. "My lip gloss must've fallen out in my cousin's car."

I dig around in my book bag and pull out my new lip gloss. "I have an extra one. You can have it."

"Oh my God, you're such a lifesaver. Are you sure?" Britney asks, smearing it on her full lips.

"Oh, yeah. No problem. I have a ton of 'em."

"Thank you *so* much. I owe you one." She pauses in thought briefly. "Actually, when's your lunch period?"

I can tell my face is getting red. Red and hot. Why is she making me so nervous? Why is she asking when my lunch period is? When *is* my lunch period? Eighth? No! Second? No! December?—grrrrr—*Get it together, April.* My mind has gone blank. *Think!*

I take a deep breath and choke out, "Fifth period."

"Mine too." Britney smiles. "Why don't you sit with me and my friends at lunch today? We can fill you in on all the hot gossip, newbie."

I can't believe my ears. She just invited me to sit at her table? Is she serious? Maybe being Britney's gym partner isn't so bad. After all, she's the conductor on the fast-track train to popularity. *Act cool, April . . . Don't let her know you're excited.*

"Definitely! Ah . . . I mean, yeah . . . sure. Really?" Okay, so I blow the cool bit.

"Sure. My family's full of philanthropicalists, and you look like a decent charity. Kisses . . ." She blows me a kiss and walks out of the locker room with the strut of an actress on the red carpet . . . leaving me utterly confused.

Philanthropicalists? I think she meant *philanthropists*. Whatever she meant, it doesn't matter at this point. What matters is that she called me a charity case, and that's just sad. All of a sudden, I find myself in a dilemma. I don't really want to sit with someone who's comparing me to the Salvation Army. But on the other hand, she's my gym partner, and I have to see her three times a week. If I don't sit with her she may be insulted, and getting on Britney Taylor's bad side is something I just can't risk.

The next few periods go by quickly, and I begin to panic during the last fifteen minutes of fourth-period math. What have I gotten myself into? What am I going to talk about? What if I trip walking up to their table? What if someone recognizes me from last year and blows my "newbie" cover? Yeah, right, who am I kidding? The only people that know me are my brother and Jeffrey Higgins, who both have lunch sixth period, King Stalker McGerk of Loserhood, who eats lunch in the library . . . and Haley, who's all the way in Kansas. I think my cover is safe.

Before I know it, the bell rings and I'm among teenage royalty in the cafeteria. It's amazing how many worshipers Britney has. She can hardly get a word in edgewise between all the flirting from vying guys.

"Jeez, Brit, they're like crazed paparazzi without the cameras," Erin, Britney's sidekick and chauffeur, says, laughing enviously.

"What do you expect? Some of them haven't seen me all summer. It'll settle down in ten minutes," Britney insists with a heavy sigh, pretending to be burdened by her good looks and popularity.

I quietly take in the circus scene surrounding the table of girls, hoping I won't have to explain how I got here. I'm clearly out of place, and feel judging eyes critiquing me from every angle. I feel like a used Honda in a Mercedes lot.

"This is Aubrey, guys. She's new."

"April. My name's April," I correct her shyly.

"Whatever." She shrugs her shoulders carelessly. "April, this is Erin, Jessica, and Brianna."

The girls stare at me coldly, seemingly unconvinced of my worthiness to sit with them. I bounce timid glances off each of them like a Ping-Pong ball.

"Hi," I say nervously. "It's nice to meet you guys."

"I know," Brianna snaps, primping her shiny auburn hair. She narrows her honey brown eyes, looking utterly annoyed by my presence.

"How did you two meet?" Erin whispers to Britney with a perplexed expression.

Britney rolls her eyes.

"In gym class. Mr. Futch paired us." She holds up the lip gloss I gave her. "April saved my lips from dehydration."

The girls glance from me to Britney to the lip gloss, still skeptical of my worthiness. I can't help but bite my lip with angst.

"Anyway." Jessica, the petite raven-haired girl sitting on Britney's left, changes the subject. "Isn't Kyle Smith looking delicious this year?"

"Yeah, but who's the girl with him?" Brianna says disparagingly.

Brit's attention immediately pans to Kyle and his new love interest. Judging from her sour expression, it pains her to see anyone else getting male attention—especially from a senior football jock.

"Ewwwwww," they exclaim in unison. "Hilary the hooker!"

"Which reminds me." Britney grins deviously. "Let's play Rank-a-Skank."

The girls clap; their eyes grow wide with excitement. I smile politely and place my hands in my lap, suddenly not knowing what to do with them.

Britney takes the lead. "How 'bout Bridget Michaels?" She points to an average-looking girl eating a pickle. "Definitely a four!"

Erin's hazy blue eyes twinkle as she nods. "Oozing with skank."

"No way. She's a five," Brianna says. "Look how she's handling that pickle!"

Everyone laughs . . . including me, even though I feel for poor, unknowing Bridget, who's just trying to enjoy her pickle in peace. Not to mention, I don't really know what I'm laughing at. Then, to my dismay, they turn to me.

"What do you think?"

Could this be more awkward? I have no clue what they're talking about, and they're asking my opinion. I'm terrified that my nerves are going to propel me to yell out something bizarre like "llama" or "gnocchi." Thankfully, my tongue lassos any looming nerd-words down as I sit motionless with a dumb deer-in-headlights kind of look.

"Well?" they say impatiently.

"Ummm," I pause to think. When in doubt, agree with the queen. "I agree with Britney. Definitely a four."

Brianna raises a dissatisfied eyebrow. "Do you even know what you're rating, April? You seem totally clueless."

My face steams up like a teakettle. I can feel sweat droplets forming in my forehead pores. She called my bluff.

"Brianna, leave her alone," Britney defends me. "Do you know how to play Rank-a-Skank, April?"

Shaking my head slightly, I mutter, "Not really."

Jessica's dark eyes glisten with thrill. "It's totally easy, April. You pick a girl and rank her on a skank scale of one to five."

Annoyed, Britney holds her hand up to Jessica's pouty lips. "Shut it! I created the game, Jess. I'll explain it."

Jessica's tanned face turns red as she recoils shamefully.

"Okay, so the skank scale is set up from one to five: one is a pinch of skank, two is a partial skank, three is a full-fledged, certified skank, four is oozing with so much skank, it's a health hazard, and five is the skunk of skanks," Britney explains.

Erin chimes in, "You need to soak in a baking-soda bath for at least three days to get the stench of a Skunk Skank off you."

I don't like the sound of this. Is this what girls do at lunch around here? I never did anything like this with Haley last year. This is way out of my comfort zone. I'd much prefer gossiping about boys and shopping.

"Okay, April, take a stab at it. Pick a skank, any skank . . . there are plenty to choose from!" Britney laughs.

Put on the spot again, not knowing what direction to look in, I immediately point to Darci Madison and her bursting chest twins sitting two tables away. After my torturous bus ride this morning, she seems like a suitable Rank-a-Skank contestant.

"Double-D Darci." Britney approves with a thoughtful nod. "Good call."

"I heard she wears a double-E bra," Erin says.

"News flash," Brit says. "She doesn't wear a bra. She wears a couple of parachutes fastened with seat belts!"

The girls laugh.

"I heard she practices frenching with her stepbrother," Jessica adds.

"Sick!" they hiss simultaneously.

"So . . ." Brianna says eagerly, indisputably enjoying the social butchering. "What d'ya rate her?"

My conscience tugs my lips shut momentarily. Yes, Darci's boobage meter is on overdrive, but I think they're being a bit harsh. I mean, she can't control her overflowing boobage meter any more than I can control my empty boobage meter. Although her revealing shirt isn't helping her cause . . . and she can definitely control her wardrobe. I hesitate for a few seconds, mediating between the envious devil and the empathetic angel on my opposing shoulders. Then, after glancing around at the four sets of expectant eyes piercing my principles, I blurt out, "She's a five. A Skunk Skank!"

I don't even know where that came from. Call it peer pressure, or succumbing to a serious case of boobicus maximus envy syndrome . . . Either way, I know it's wrong . . . and I'm not proud of it.

"Aw—she's caught on!" Britney beams with pride. "I love having naive newbies around. I'm a teacher at heart, y'know."

Before long, the girls turn their criticism to a stylish, pretty blonde in the corner of the cafeteria. Wait a second—I recognize her. That's Melanie Elmer. Why are they talking bad about her? I thought she was best friends with these girls. Melanie and Britney seemed inseparable last year. In fact, I thought they were sisters until Haley informed me otherwise. Obviously I can't say anything. Since they think I just moved here, I shouldn't know this.

"She totally deserves to eat alone," Britney says callously. "She's not even worth our insults."

For the rest of lunch, Britney and her partners in crime saturate me with gossip, enlighten me with fashion tips, fill me in on who's hot and who's not, and even teach me some of their lingo. I know for a fact that I never want to be called a meatball packer (fatty), chumpnut (hopeless idiot), nerd herder (king of nerds), scag (crusty like a scab and ugly like a hag), or freak funnel (outcast), among other things.

In addition, I find out that Erin is Britney's cousin ("Second cousin!" Britney is quick to point out). Erin also reveals that she's obsessed with spray tanning. No surprise there. Her orange-marbled palms are evidence that she hasn't quite gotten the gist of an even tan yet. At least I know I'm not the only one at the table with a shallow addiction.

By the end of the period, my head is clogged with so much superficial static, it's practically seeping from my ears. I'm actually pleased to get a break from the group when Britney suggests that I dump the garbage.

"Every newcomer has to throw out our lunches. It's like the first rite of passage or something. Really, it's a compliment."

"Wait, I'm not done." Erin scarfs down a few more Tater Tots.

"Tater Tots are repulsive. Pure thigh stuffers. Remember Law Three, Erin. You better watch it!" Britney scolds.

Whatever Law Three is, it must mean something to Erin. She quickly puts down the greasy bites and tops the garbage pile with her half-eaten tray of food. Before I venture to the large trash cans, Jessica notices my uneaten lunch.

"You didn't even eat, April. I totally get you. You're just like me. I stuck to a diet of raw veggies and Diet Cokes for a whole month this summer until my mom forced me to go to a nutritionist," she says, pinching her nonexistent belly.

I nod and smile as if she's spot on. Really, though, I'm not dieting . . . not even close. The truth is that I was too stressed to eat all period. The last thing I want is for the girls to critique how I put food in my mouth, lecture me on calorie intake, or laugh at ketchup on my face. They definitely aren't the kind of friends that would subtly tell me to use my napkin. Although I'm sitting where tons of girls yearn to be, I've felt like I'm going to throw up this whole time.

However, the rush of adrenaline I get from my walk to the trash can is amazing. I'm checked out by every other guy I pass and whispered about reverently by multiple groups of girls. Really, I don't know if they're admiring me, or curious about all the garbage I'm carrying . . . but either way, I've gone from a boring nothing to an interesting something just by sitting with these girls. This flattering attention is almost worth the social slaughter I've just contributed to.

I dump the trash and turn around like a model to start my catwalk-stroll back. I look up, and I'm instantly love-struck! Mr. Hottie-Body Brentwood is staring me up and down. How had I not noticed him this whole time? *Act cool, April . . . Act cool!* But how can I walk with a master of hotness watching me? My knees buckle. I start to panic. Then I remember, hey, I'm sitting with school celebrities; why wouldn't he be staring? This bolt of confidence gives me the boost I need to walk my best strut yet. He smiles as I walk by, and I get up the nerve to speak.

"Hi." Okay, so it isn't Shakespeare or anything, but give me a break—I made the first move.

"Hey," he says, showing his delicious smile.

I almost faint . . . but I don't. I want to sit on his lap, run my fingers through his thick, scruffy brown hair, and lick his face from top to bottom. *Say something else, April . . . open dialogue!* I can't. Words escape me. So, I decide that the next best thing to do is to leave him wanting more. I walk away with my heart pounding like a rock concert all the way back to the table, wondering if he's watching my butt.

"She has total puppet potential," I overhear Britney say as I sit back down. The girls smile at me with plastic grins of acceptance.

"What?"

"Oh, nothing. Who's that hottie you were ogling at over there?"

"Oh!" I'm caught off-guard. Ogling? Oh, gosh, had it been that obvious? "He's nobody. Just some guy in my homeroom. His name's Matthew."

I don't trust them enough to let them know that he's my future husband and I've renamed him Mr. Hottie-Body Brentwood.

"Nobody? He doesn't look like a nobody! You were practically drooling over him." Brianna snickers.

I want to stick my head into the ground like an ostrich to hide. I had been so proud of my femme fatale act . . . but it seems as though I was the opposite—a drooling, ogling mess.

"You—have—a—crush!" Erin singsongs like a second-grader.

"Not really," I say nervously. "Well, I just think he's hot, that's all. No big deal."

"You're pretty *and* you have good taste in guys."

I smile bashfully, astonished that Britney Taylor, the princess of pretty, thinks I'm pretty, too.

She continues, "It's like you're a mini-me or something . . . just slightly bigger. Which, I guess would actually make you a jumbo-me, but whatever."

I instantly feel huge and self-conscious. I'm glad that I didn't eat my lunch.

"We won't tell anyone, April," Britney adds, sliding her freshly manicured finger over her mouth like a zipper. "Your secret is our secret."

"Thanks," I say, knowing full well that I can't trust a girl who created the Rank-a-Skank game.

chapter three

After a torturous ninth-period history class with the dreaded Mr. Stuart, I can't rush home quickly enough. Flinging open the door of home sweet home, I immediately race Aaden to the phone. "I've got dibs," I yell as I slide across the kitchen floor to wrest the phone from him. He always does this. He never even gives me time to run to the phone in my room. If we both hadn't lost our cells last week, this wouldn't even be an issue right now.

"When you learn not to rack your bill up to the moon, you can have it back," my dad said heartlessly when he took my life force away five days, twenty-one hours, and forty-four minutes ago.

"Aaden, let your sister use the phone," my mom calls from the other room.

"Why do you always side with her?" the mole shouts.

"You saw your friends today in school; she didn't. I want to hear how your first day was when you get off the phone, April."

My brother snarls, grudgingly handing over the phone. Knowing that going out with Jeffrey "Goat Boy" Higgins this weekend is dependent on his behavior this week really works to my advantage.

"If you hadn't been such a tool for the last month, maybe you'd still have your cell," I growl at him as I dial.

"Back at you," he grunts.

My heart feels like it's going to jump out of my chest when the phone starts ringing.

"Hello?"

"Haley!"

"Hey! So—"

I cut her off. There's no time for opening chitchat. She doesn't start school for another week, so this is my time to talk. "I met the guy of my dreams!"

I see my mom curiously peek her head around the corner of her office. I'm sure that's the last thing she was expecting to hear. I quickly run upstairs to my room to get some much-needed privacy.

"Back the truck up. What? Where—"

"Oh my gosh, Lee! You would die! You would absolutely melt to the floor and drain through the cracks if you saw this guy!"

"Who—"

"He's new. Totally hot! He's my spring formal date . . . he just doesn't know it yet."

"Spring formal? That's not until May. Aren't you jumping ahead of yourself a little?"

"Maybe, but you don't understand. He's so hot, I have to lay my claim early or someone might steal him away."

"What's his name?"

"Matthew Brentwood . . . but I've renamed him Mr. Hottie-Body Brentwood, and you're talking to the future Mrs. Hottie-Body Brentwood."

She laughs. "What? No way! You mean you've gotten over King Stalker McGerk? But you guys made such a cute couple."

"Ugh! Very funny," I say. "Get this—so, Delvin's in my science class, and he stared at me from bell to bell. I could feel his radar eyes burning a hole in my cheek. It was unbearable. Restraining order is all I have to say . . . but back to Hottie-Body—"

"How'd you meet?"

"Well, we haven't officially met yet. I admired him in Satan's homeroom. And we said hi to each other at lunch."

"Satan's homeroom?"

"Mr. Stuart's my homeroom teacher *and* my ninth-period history teacher. What are the chances of beginning and ending every school day in hell? Obviously, someone in the scheduling department is trying to kill me."

"Stu-man is terrifying!" Haley sympathizes. "So, you talked to this Matthew kid in lunch today? Who'd you sit with?"

I pause for a second, remembering Haley's disdain for Britney. I have to tell her, though. I hope she won't be mad at me. "You'll never believe this, Lee; I sat at Brit Taylor's table."

Silence.

"Lee?"

"How did *that* happen?" she asks.

"Honestly, I don't really know. We were paired up in gym class and I gave her lip gloss . . . and then she invited me to sit with them. Weird, isn't it?"

Silence.

I know she disapproves. Haley is never silent. "It's not what you think. It was sort of awkward . . . but—"

She breaks her silence. "Oh, April, be careful! Don't get wrapped up with them!"

"What d'ya mean?"

"Britney is *not* a nice girl. You can't trust her!"

"Who said I trust her?"

"It's not just her . . . it's all of them."

"Just 'cause I sat with them today doesn't mean I'm all buddy-buddy with them. They're sorta snobby. Except Jessica seems pretty cool," I say, remembering how nice she was in our sixth-period Spanish class.

"Snobby is an understatement. You just need to stay away from that whole group. Seriously. Don't you remember what I told you about them?"

"I remember," I say vaguely. I know they had a big falling out, but Haley never seemed to want to talk about the details. All I know is that Britney is Haley's nemesis, and I fully understand why she's upset right now. But, come on, what does she expect from me? It's not like I could pass up a seat at the popular table to sit by myself. I add, "But I didn't have a choice. It was my only seating option."

"I highly doubt that," she grumbles. "You'd be better off sitting next to a tub of coleslaw with the lunch ladies. Britney Taylor is the ringleader of evil, and her friends are her evil circus clowns!"

I laugh. "Well then, I promise that I'll never turn into one of her evil circus clowns. I'm afraid of clowns, remember? Anyway, Brit didn't seem that bad. She was actually pretty nice to me . . . until she called me a jumbo-me."

"What?"

"Long story."

"Look, you know how I feel about her; I don't need to repeat myself. You're too nice to be friends with them. You can't let them suck you in," Haley says with a distinct parent-like tone. "Just be careful. And whatever you do, stay far away from red lipstick."

Red lipstick? What does that have to do with anything? My curiosity tempts me to ask what she's talking about, but I quickly decide not to press her for more info. She seems irritable enough at this point, and I know all things involving Britney Taylor are sore subjects for Haley. There's definitely bad blood there, and it's just easier to agree and try to change the subject.

"Okay," I say.

Sensing her immense concern, I specifically forget to mention that I've already accepted Brit's invitation to sit with them at lunch again tomorrow. Instead, I say, "Don't worry—my best friend moved to Wichita, Kansas, and no one can replace her!"

"Awww—I miss ya, Apes!" Haley sighs.

"Miss you too, Lee."

I get off the phone with her, and to my horror, my brother is rustling around outside my door.

"Someone's got a homeroom crush. Wait till Mr. Hottie-Body gets the good news!" he yells through the crack.

Can he be any more juvenile? No, he can't. It's hard to believe he's a year older than me. I burst my door open to confront the jerk. "If you say anything, I'll kill you, Aaden!"

Later that night, I have a horrible nightmare. I dream that I'm half-naked, in my underwear and tissue-stuffed bra, standing on a cafeteria table. Britney is circling fat patches on my body with red lipstick, and her friends are all taunting and laughing at me. Mr. Hottie-Body Brentwood and the rest of my class-mates surround me, looking totally repulsed.

Haley's voice screeches over the school loudspeaker: "I warned you!"

I wake up completely panicked. Understandably, I can't get back to sleep for quite a while.

The next day in homeroom, I'm livid when I catch a glimpse of my brother approaching Matthew. I strain my ears to hear what he's saying, but the whole homeroom is way too loud for me to overhear their conversation. I pout quietly at my desk. I can feel my face turn red, and I want to dissolve into my chair. I can only imagine the lies he's making up to embarrass me.

Mr. Stuart marches in. The room becomes silent, and every-one scampers to their desks, including my brother. Hopefully he didn't have time to mortify me too much.

"Well, well . . . much better today!" He dishes out a rare compliment. "Time for attendance."

Going into my own little world, I try to figure out how I'll explain to Matthew that I'm not a complete lunatic. I'm sure that whatever my brother told him made me sound beyond nutso. I'm swept up in my sulking when I realize Mr. Stuart is staring right at me and has called my name for the third time.

"Oh! Sorry. I'm here." I raise my hand, more embarrassed than ever.

"Your body is here, but your brain isn't. Is that right, Miss Bowers?"

The class laughs. I'm humiliated. This day is getting better and better.

By the time the bell rings for first period, I've riled myself up into a minor panic attack. On the outside, I'm trying to appear normal, but on the inside I'm in the midst of a meltdown. As I gather my books to head out, I smell something familiarly delicious. I'm stunned when I look up to see Matthew standing over me, smiling. The shine from his bright white teeth temporarily blinds me. I jump involuntarily, losing my grip, and my books scatter everywhere.

"Oh, sorry . . . I—I . . ." I trip over my nervous tongue, scrambling to pick my books up.

He helps me gather them. "No, I'm sorry, April. Didn't mean to scare you."

Jackpot! He knows my name! My cheeks stretch to accommodate a huge smile. I stare giddily, mesmerized by his scrumptious lips.

"You okay?" he says.

I realize that I'm not helping my cause by acting ridiculously smitten. "Yeah, sorry . . . just, just thinking."

Just *thinking?* What kind of a response is that? What is wrong with me?

"Right, I guess that's what school's for." He laughs awkwardly. "You mind if I walk you to your next class?"

"Sure . . . I mean, no, no . . . I don't mind." April, for the love of all things holy, *get it together!*

We proceed into the bustling hallway, and I try to start a normal conversation. "So, your name's Matthew, right?" I ask, relieved that I sound halfway normal.

"You can call me Matt."

I smile. "So, where'd you move from, Matt?"

"Erie, Pennsylvania," he says.

"Get out!" I say ecstatically. "We were practically neighbors. I'm from Pittsburgh originally. I lived in the South Hills. I still miss it."

"No way. What are the chances? A cute girl like you and a cool guy like me ending up in the same school." He winks.

Wait a second . . . Did he just call me cute? Not only that, but did he just wink at me, too? Am I hallucinating? I soon realize that I'm smiling aimlessly, like I'm jacked up on happy pills, surely looking like a clinically diagnosed loon. I have to say something quickly to save me from appearing like a lieutenant of loserhood.

The desperate words "Must be fate" slip from my mouth before I have a chance to stop them. I bite my lip and glance over at him, hoping he doesn't think I'm cheesy.

Thankfully, he seems receptive.

"Or luck." He smiles. "Is this your first year here, too?"

"No, I moved last year." Crap—did I just say that? I hope that doesn't get back to Britney. I quickly change the subject. "You're probably a Steelers fan, right?" Good save; no guy can resist talking about football.

"Of course. You?"

"Yep," I respond, hoping he forgets my previous comment.

Standing outside my art class, I summon the nerve to ask, "So, what was my brother saying to you in homeroom?"

"Oh yeah, that," he says. "He didn't really have time to say much. He just told me you have something really funny to tell me. So, do you?"

"Funny? Hmm . . ." My annoying brother tried to set me up

to look like an idiot! "Aaden's not the sharpest tool in the shed. He doesn't know what he's talking about half of the time. But maybe, if you're lucky, I'll think of a joke to make you laugh the next time I see you."

I try to seduce him with my smile, proud of the magic that's coming out of my mouth.

"I'm gonna hold you to that, April," he says. "Have a good art class."

"Thanks!"

The butterflies in my stomach feel like they're about to burst out to paint the room with rainbows. Thank you, Aaden! Little does my brother know that his attempt to embarrass me backfired. Ha! I sit down at an art table, pleased with my performance. I begin counting down the minutes until I see Matt next. In the meantime, I have to think of something funny to tell him.

By the time lunch period rolls around, I've remembered a Cleveland Browns joke that no Steelers fan can deny. I walk cheerfully into the cafeteria. I can't wait to see Matt. He'll think I'm a football comedy genius.

I instantly see Britney waving me over to sit with her. Part of me feels disloyal to Haley, but a bigger part of me feels like the coolest girl in school. Which, after my dismal freshman year, is pretty much a dream come true.

"'Sup, girlie?" She greets me with a smile.

"Hi!" I sit down confidently. Even after Haley's warning and my terrible nightmare, I feel so much more comfortable sitting at her table today. Britney's being super friendly, and the other girls seem surprisingly welcoming. Things couldn't be going any better. The gossip and fashion talk begin immediately.

As Brianna is halfway through her theory on why buying clothes from a designer discount outlet is a travesty, I feel a strong hand on my shoulder. I turn around breathlessly, anticipating a flirt fiesta.

"Hi, Matt!" I gush with a huge grin. A shock of adoration fills my body as I gaze at his perfect face.

The girls watch in awe. He's definitely the hottest sophomore at Penford High School, and I'm the only one at the table who knows him! This totally skyrockets my popularity potential in their eyes. I'm sure of it.

"So, I think you have something to tell me," Matt says flirtatiously.

I'm so glad he remembered. I quickly prepare myself to tell the masterful joke.

Right as I open my mouth to say it, Britney interrupts me. "I have something to tell you . . . You're a hottie!"

She pulls her elbows together under the lunch table, making her already-deep cleavage monstrous.

"Thanks." He blushes. "You aren't so bad yourself!"

I'm seething with jealousy. I feel searing steam coming out of my ears. I try to hide the fact that I'm a raging bull, but it's nearly impossible. I want to claw her eyes out for ruining my big moment. I can't recover from this. I slowly see the situation turning into a Britney and Matt flirt festival. It's nauseating.

After he walks away, Britney smiles at me smugly. "I think he's *totally* into you."

I bear a fake grin and begrudgingly say, "You think?"

"Oh, yeah! No doubt!" The rest of the girls chime in, trying to save Brit's backstabbing face. "He's *totally* into you!"

"Anyway"—Britney points to Brianna—"what were you saying before he came over?"

And the whole Matt Brentwood ordeal is dropped. Brianna continues her trivial discussion, Britney resumes her superior poses, and I pretend to get over it. However, I tuck the incident in the back of my mind as one point scored for Haley's team.

chapter four

Despite Britney's flirt filching antics earlier this week, I accept an invitation to go to her house over the weekend. After all, I'm not stupid enough to let boy jealousy get in the way of a potential social life. Plus, I couldn't wait to see her house.

I'm shocked when my mom drops me off. From how much Brit brags about having money, I was expecting her to live in a grandiose mansion upon acres of beautifully landscaped rolling hills. Instead, she lives in a tiny two-bedroom townhouse with her mom. Her development looks more like a bunch of cereal boxes shoved together snugly on a grocery store shelf than a neighborhood. The only hint of wealth is the new red BMW parked in her narrow stone driveway.

It doesn't take long for me to regret my decision to hang out with her when I find myself in her small, gaudy bedroom in the midst of a makeover intervention. No girl wants to hear that she needs a makeover. I know I'm not a supermodel, but c'mon, I'm not a wilting weed in desperate need of Miracle-Gro, either.

"What's wrong?" she says, analyzing my thwarted expression. "You didn't think I was inviting you over for a tea party, did you?"

"No," I say. "I just didn't think I'd be getting a makeover today."

"You're a friend in training right now. Consider this part of your orientation," she says sharply. "It's a compliment."

Britney Taylor is a master of twisting insults into "compliments." I feel a tinge of ego pain resonating from my toes and slowly traveling up my body. Not only have I been made abruptly aware that I need a makeover, now I'm told I'm a friend in training. It's not that I'm desperate for Britney's friendship and approval . . . Okay, on second thought, maybe I am a little . . . because making friends is on the top of my list at this point. And although I know from Haley's warning that Britney may not be the best friend to make, sitting with her at lunch this week has been a huge ego booster. And my ego has been in dire need of boosting for quite a while now.

"So, let's get started!" she says, rubbing her hands together with a devilish look in her eyes. She pulls me over in front of the large mirror above her dresser. Two sequined pink lamps are bordering both sides of the dresser, and the mirror is adorned with several pink feather boas. I feel dizzy from all the pink. Not to mention, I'm allergic to feathers. My sinuses bulge and stuff immediately.

She points to my reflection and says, "Do you know what's wrong with this picture?"

I suddenly feel disconnected from my body. As if I'm evaluating a random painting in some stuffy museum. I've never been good at subjective critiques . . . and I'm finding it even harder now that the subject is me. Don't get me wrong; I have plenty of flaws that I'm aware of. The trouble is, I don't feel comfortable pointing them out in front of the most beautiful girl in tenth grade.

"I'm confused," I say between sinus sniffles. "Just the other day, you said I was pretty."

"You are pretty," she says. "You're just not applying your prettiness properly."

"What do you mean, not applying my prettiness?"

"It's the whole package. It doesn't add up," she says, shaking her head, her arms crossed tightly.

I glance into the mirror with a confused expression. I notice that my eyes are a bit bloodshot and my nose is turning red from the boas. I'm quickly reminded of Haley's evil circus clown comment. However, I'm much more interested in Britney's critique right now. She's gorgeous and probably knows what she's talking about in this arena.

Britney explains, "You see, it's like an addition problem. Every number adds up to the total sum. Everything about you from your shoes to your hair is a number. The total sum is your prettiness factor. You want the highest possible number for each separate part to add up to the highest possible prettiness factor total."

I'm shocked by how smart she sounds. On the contrary, I know for a fact (from sitting a few seats behind Britney in math class last year) that math is not her forte.

"It's like a mathemalogical equation-ish thingy," she adds with a confident smile.

I look at her like she's speaking a foreign language.

"Let me give you an example," she says. "If I wore a muumuu every day of the week, I wouldn't be applying my skinniness properly. No one would notice my skinniness factor because I wouldn't be showing it."

I begin to have a headache . . . not sure if it's due to the feathers or to Britney's voice.

She continues, "For you, no one can see your prettiness factor because . . ." She pauses. "Well, you just don't stand out. Nothing screams 'April has entered the building!'"

I look at her quizzically, not quite sure if I want to scream "April has entered the building."

Britney sighs. "You see, your hair, makeup, clothes . . . It's all blah. You're not *applying* your prettiness. Get it?"

"Yes," I assert, still partially confused. "Do you think I should straighten my hair?"

This is something I've contemplated for several years. I've always loathed my curls and longed for straight hair. I secretly hope that Britney will agree that straightening my hair will fix everything.

"Not necessarily," she says with her finger up in prime lecture position. "Believe it or not, curly hair is coming back in."

"Really?" I ask incredulously, then sneeze. She hands me a tissue. A look of disapproval crosses her face as I blow my stuffed nose.

"Yeah, don't ask me why." She rolls her eyes. "Anyhow, you're ahead of the hair trend, so I don't think you should straighten; I just think you should tone it down a bit."

"How?" I say, hoping for a miracle answer. I've tried every product on the market to make my hair less . . . pouffy. I'd love to tone down my pouffiness factor.

"We'll buy a diffuser and frizz serum at the mall."

"Okay," I say doubtfully. I blow my nose again. This, of course, is met by another look of disgust from Britney.

I smile apologetically, and she continues. "Moving on to your makeup . . ."

"What's wrong with it?"

"What's not?" She laughs.

The tinge of ego pain emanates through my body again.

"First, I can tell you buy cheap makeup," she says. "Second, I can see your makeup."

"Isn't that what it's for? So people can see it?" I say.

"Yes and no." She puts her finger up again. "Makeup should be subtle enough to go unnoticed. It should enhance, not mask. I mean, look at your eyes . . . You have awesome blue eyes, but they don't pop at all behind all that cheap makeup."

"Right," I say, thinking it's easier to agree than debate. "Are you going to teach me how to do my makeup?"

"I'm not," she says. "My mom is."

"Your mom?" I say, quickly followed by a sniffle, sniffle, sneeze, and blow.

After another look of repulsion, Britney says, "Yeah, she's a Chanel makeup artist at Macy's. You have an appointment with her in an hour."

"I do?" My nerves rev up. Mainly because I don't like random people touching my face, thank you very much.

"Yep, so . . . we should move along here," she says hastily. "Now for your clothes."

"What's wrong with my clothes? I love shopping!" I say, taking offense.

"Exactly!" she says. "I can tell that you love shopping . . . in the clearance racks. Not only that, I can tell that on the rare occasions you're not buying clearance, you buy everything off of a store mannequin."

I grab another tissue and move away from the feather boa culprits as I process what she's said. She's spot on. How does she know all this? I do love good sales. Doesn't everyone? And

I do get outfit ideas from the mannequin displays. But what's wrong with that? Isn't that what the mannequin displays are for . . . to guide shoppers on what looks good together?

"You're too commercial," she adds. "My friends need to make the trends, not follow them."

"Okay," I say. "But what's wrong with good sales?"

"Some sales are fine. Like buy-one-get-one-half-off sales or holiday discounts. Those are good. But stay away from the clearance racks. They're last season's rejects. It's like a crime scene. You don't want your fingerprints anywhere near a clearance rack. One wrong buy will land you with the fashion police."

I have a suspicion that Britney considers herself a chief fashion police officer.

She proceeds with her lecture. "All of my friends need a fashion niche to stand out. Brianna has sophisticated, expensive taste. She's my designer fashionista friend. Jessica has trendy taste. She's my trend inventor friend. And Erin . . . well—"

"She's a hippie chick, right? She likes flowy clothes," I say, hoping to impress her with my keen fashion observation . . . and, in turn, distract from my sinus spasms.

"No accounting for taste." Britney laughs. "She only wears that stuff 'cause she's too big to be trendy."

Ugh . . . I feel a stab in the heart for Erin. That's an awful thing to say about anyone—whether it's true or not. But in Erin's case, it's definitely not true. She has a flawless body like the rest of them. Maybe compared to Britney, she isn't petite . . . but no one, except for Jessica, is petite next to Britney. I glare in the mirror critically, wondering if Britney thinks I'm fat. I feel like a huge, ugly beast next to her after all this talk about prettiness and skinniness factors.

"So, what do you want your niche to be?"

"My what?" I ask—I've forgotten what we were talking about while comparing myself to a large ogre.

"Your fashion niche? What do you want it to be?" she says impatiently.

"Oh . . . I dunno," I say, scraping my brain for any possible idea that sounds halfway decent. "Maybe . . . uh . . . maybe I'll be a pairer?"

"A what?" she says critically. "What does *a pairer* mean?"

"Um . . . ummm . . ." I scramble for a definition, as I have no idea what it means myself. "I—um . . . I'll pair new and old trends together to make innovative trends?" I say, sounding like a fool. I'm totally bluffing and am sure Britney's going to destroy me.

Instead, she exclaims, "That's a great idea!"

"It *is?*" I say, perplexed. Did she understand what I said? Because I didn't.

"Yeah! I never thought of that before. You could totally create new trends by putting random trends together that aren't usually paired. It's so fashion forward."

Oh, no. I can picture it now—me walking around in a hodgepodge trendy mess all in the name of my "pairer" fashion niche. I can hardly wait to show up at school wearing a fedora hat, Ugg boots, and a Juicy Couture tracksuit topped with a wide waist belt. Just call me fashion Frankenstein. What have I gotten myself into?

"I'll get you started!" Britney says intently, retreating into her overflowing closet.

"I don't think I'll fit in your clothes," I say, partly because it's true, and partly because I don't want to wear a ridiculous outfit to the mall.

"Sure you will," she says, her voice muffled by fabric. "You're not *that* much bigger than me."

A smile widens on my face. Britney thinks I can fit in her clothes. This statement makes me happy, regardless of my fashion Frankenstein future. Gloating, I gaze around her room, taking in all the glitter, sequins, and pink. A large red chair in the corner of her room sticks out like a sore thumb against all the pink. It's shaped like a giant high-heeled shoe. It looks unreasonably uncomfortable and awkward.

My attention then pans to Britney's bed. The pink comforter and silk sheets are crumpled together sloppily. For a girl who seems so neurotically obsessed with order in fashion, looks, and weight, she sure keeps an untidy bed. I notice a pink binder on her bedside table and immediately wonder what's in it. I make sure that Britney is still busy figuring out what crazy outfit to put me in before walking over to check it out.

The words THE LIPSTICK LAWS are scrolled over the front of the binder in fancy red cursive. Lipstick? I wonder if this is what Haley was warning me about . . . I have to snoop! My hands are sweaty with anticipation as I open it to sneak a peek.

"What are you doing?" Britney interrupts my nosiness harshly.

I shut the binder quickly, knocking a framed picture of her and the girls off of the bedside table.

"Nothing," I say unconvincingly, reaching to pick up the picture.

Britney throws the outfit she's holding on her bed. She stomps over to me, her lips twisted in a scowl. She snatches the binder away and says, "This is off-limits! Like I said, you're a friend in training. You're still in the application phase. You haven't gotten the position yet. You won't see this again until you get the job!" She shoves the binder in a dresser drawer and closes it. "*If* you get the job," she adds with a sneer.

"I'm sorry, Britney. I wasn't trying to snoop. I promise," I fib, feeling embarrassed. At the same time, my curiosity about the Lipstick Laws spikes. What could they be? What could she be guarding so fiercely?

Britney continues to stare me down abrasively. Feeling increasingly uncomfortable, I put the framed picture back in place and try to change the subject. "You guys look so pretty in this picture."

She walks closer to me and evaluates the framed photograph. I've noticed that giving Britney a compliment is a sure way to shift her focus.

She smiles and says, "I know, right? I've got all my bases covered."

"Bases?" I say, confused by her response.

"Yeah. My friendship bases. I have a wealthy friend for VIP status," she says, pointing to Brianna. "A pretty friend for healthy competition." She points to Jessica. "And an ugly friend to always make me look better." She grins and points to Erin.

"But Erin's pretty!" I blurt impulsively. It's crazy to think anyone in Britney's exclusive clique is anything less than gorgeous.

"Trust me—she's not. You've never seen her without makeup. Besides, haven't you noticed that she looks like a ripened orange?" she responds snidely.

How could Britney say that about her own cousin? Yeah, she's slightly addicted to self tanning, but that doesn't make her ugly. She's far from ugly. If Britney says this about Erin behind her back, I don't even want to begin to think about what she says about me. I glance at her warily. "Why would you say that? Do you not like Erin or something?"

"Just because she's ugly doesn't mean I don't like her. God, I'm not *that* superficial." She rolls her eyes. "She's my cousin. I have to like her . . . But honestly, I wouldn't be friends with her if we weren't related. Oh well . . . You can't pick your family, right?"

A loud car horn honks outside before I have time to answer.

"Speaking of the orange devil," Britney says brightly, peering out her window. "That's her. She's taking us to the mall. Guess you won't have time to change."

A sigh of relief comes over me as I pass the horrendous fashion Frankenstein outfit she picked out for me strewn over her messy bed.

~⊙~

Once we get to the mall, Erin circles the parking lot, searching for the perfect parking space. Britney decides to use this time to "enlighten" me some more.

"I need to show you our MPOA before we get out," she says firmly, reaching into her Coach tote.

"What's an MPOA?" I ask.

"Mall Plan of Attack," Erin says, making eye contact with me through the rearview mirror.

Britney hands me a copy of the Eastview Mall directory. She's scribbled all over it with a red pen and yellow highlighter.

"As you can see," she directs me, "there are large red *X*s over restricted areas. Low-end department stores, drugstores, Gothic stores, dollar stores, and the arcade are all off-limits. Also, keep in mind that the food court is strictly for meatball packers. You should never be within a ten-foot radius of any of these areas."

"Okay," I say, thinking this is bizarre. "So, if I can't go in these areas, where can I go?"

"Stick with the stores highlighted in yellow," she responds quickly.

"I see," I say, pretending to study the map before handing it back to Britney.

"No, no," she says. "That's your copy. Keep it. You need it more than I do."

"Thanks," I say halfheartedly, folding it into my purse.

Before long, I'm being painted with various makeup brushes in the middle of Macy's by Britney's lookalike mom. She explains that I have a "great canvas" and that I just need to learn to "paint like Picasso instead of a preschooler." I see where Britney gets her backhanded compliments from.

When she's finished with her masterpiece, she hands me a mirror proudly.

"Take a look," she says. "You're going to love it."

I can't stop staring at my face. Is it mine? Okay, maybe Britney was right. This new look makes a big difference. I look drop-dead . . . Mr. Hottie-Body won't be able to resist me! Hopefully I'll be able to reproduce it on my own. In the meantime, I can't wait to see Brit's and Erin's reactions. They took off twenty minutes ago to prowl the store. I wonder if they'll even recognize me . . .

"Well, what do you think?" Brit's mom looks at me with an air of conceit. "Isn't it fabulous?"

I nod in disbelief. "I love it!"

"And . . . the best part is, it's all yours."

"What's all mine?" I say.

"The makeup. Everything we used today is yours. Consider it a present from Britney."

"Oh my gosh! Thank you so much!" I beam as she gathers it all into a Chanel makeup bag.

"You're welcome, April. As a makeup artist, my job is to help people in cosmetic need, so consider yourself helped." She smiles sympathetically at me.

My face drops cheerlessly. Cosmetic need? What the heck does that mean? Wow, Britney really does take after her mom. Anyhow, I can't let that bother me. I look fab-tastic and should be celebrating, not pouting. And that's exactly what I do when the girls return, in complete awe of my transformation.

"Now we just need to tone down your Medusa mop top and you'll be good to go," Britney says, pointing to my hair.

I'm too happy about my new makeup to be upset that she's bashing my hair. If she can spread the magic to my hair that her mom used on my face, I may just be a knockout by the time the day is done. Fingers crossed.

We spend the rest of the day shopping, getting mani- and pedicures, and gossiping. I know Britney says I'm just a friend in training, but it really feels good to have people to hang out with again. Especially people who warrant stares from cute boys and jealous girls. If this gets me a social life worth socializing about, maybe I can put up with Brit's brattiness. I mean, she's the reason I have a hot new look and stocked makeup bag. Maybe, just maybe, Haley was wrong. Maybe Britney Taylor isn't that bad.

chapter five

Unfortunately, after a few more weeks of being too close for comfort to the popularity princess, I find that Haley was right. Britney Taylor *is* that bad. But not only am I indebted to her for giving me a stellar makeover, I've also found that the fame of hanging out with her is too enticing to pass up. So, even though she's a certified nightmare, I don't want to wake from this popularity dream anytime soon.

My only problem is that I haven't talked to Haley in what seems like forever. I know she's annoyed that I'm hanging out with Britney. Plus, Haley's new boyfriend isn't making it any easier for me to get a hold of her. She's always with him. If I could talk to her, though, she would be glad to hear that I secretly despise Britney. But I'd be crazy to abandon Brit's rock star group for . . . well . . . nobody. At this point, hiding my feelings of disdain for her is second nature—almost as easy as breathing. No one would ever suspect that I pray every night for her to lose her hair in a dreadful Nair hair-removal accident. If only I could devise a foolproof plan to switch out her shampoo with the balding butter.

Her constant nagging demands are getting on my last nerve. She has next-to-impossible standards for her friends:

- "Don't chew your gum like that, Jessica! It makes you look like total white trash."

- "Erin, you look like an orange tie-dyed freak funnel with that crap on your skin. You need to fix it!"
- "Your ears are too big to wear your hair up, Bri, remember?"
- "April, your boobs look deformed today. You really need to readjust your bra."

Little does she know that readjusting means emptying, re-fluffing, and restuffing like a pillow in a pillowcase. She'd die if she found out that my plump boob buds are stuffed like a Thanksgiving turkey.

Britney also has pretty brutal fashion tips:

- "Take off that belt, Brianna. You look like a meatball packer!"
- "Erin, you can so not pull off skinny jeans. You have to be skinny to do that."
- "Stop shopping clearance, April. Your whole wardrobe probably cost you twelve fifty. It's a total fashion crime."
- "That shirt should be illegal, Jessica. On a hideousness scale of one to ten, it's a fifteen."

Britney also loves to put negative twists on anyone else's good news:

- "Nick Malbo likes you, Jess? Yeah, he's hot . . . but there's a reason his nickname is Bo. He stinks like a trucker."
- "Bri, just because you're moving into a seventy-five-hundred-square-foot house doesn't mean you're special."
- "Erin, you lost the five pounds you're bragging about in your boobs. I guess you'll need to get some new bras the next time we're at the mall."
- "Don't feel too proud for getting an A on your English

paper, April. Mr. Bilsby gives out As as much as Darci Madison swaps spit in the boys' bathroom."

And she is always so right . . . even when she is obviously *so* wrong:

- "Hawaii is so not a state, Jessica—God, how dumb can you be?"
- "April, conceited is a compliment, not an insult."
- "Please, Brianna, go back to first grade spelling. There's no A in beautiful."
- "Keep going, Erin; a flashing red light means proceed with caution, not stop! Didn't you learn anything from your driving test?"

Hence Erin's first traffic ticket for a rolling stop. Britney still claims that the cop was so wrong. "He was probably a total turd in high school and likes to take revenge on popular, pretty girls. We should seriously report him."

Brit is the last person who should be directing anyone on driving. She turned sixteen in August and has already failed her driving test three times. Yet she still believes she knows everything about driving, along with every other subject known to man. Ugh! She's a vile, self-obsessed, know-it-all happiness ruiner, to put it lightly. Unfortunately, not only am I addicted to bosom sculpting, I am now also shamefully addicted to the celebrity that goes along with being seen with Britney Taylor.

"I should call my mom to let her know I'll be a little late," I say in the back of Erin's red Neon.

"Use your cell," Jessica yells over the blasting music.

"Remember, my parents took it away this summer," I yell back.

Britney turns down the music. "Let her worry about you. She deserves it. It's her fault you don't have your cell. She shouldn't get mad if you can't call."

"You won't be that long, anyhow. You're just signing the Lipstick Oath. It will take a half hour tops," Brianna says.

My heart is beating rapidly, remembering Haley's weird warning about lipstick. I'm wondering if this Lipstick Oath is what she was referring to. I wish she hadn't left me in the dark. Furthermore, I wish I had been able to accomplish a more thorough snoop of that pink Lipstick Laws binder in Britney's room. This oath must have something to do with it.

I try to calm my nerves . . . How bad can it be? Supposedly, it's some big honor and final rite of passage into their group. Britney explained it as a promotion from a "friend in training" to a "certified friend." I'm not half as excited as she says I should be. I don't trust Britney, and wouldn't put it past her to think up some imprisonment game where I'm locked in a closet for a week and forced to eat nothing but lipstick. My mouth becomes dry and gummy just thinking about it.

We pull up to Britney's cereal-box development. She's clearly in denial about the size of her house. This wouldn't even matter if she wasn't such a bling bragger. Erin made me promise not to tell Britney that I know Britney's father is the only one with money . . . and he left six years ago to start a new family with some chick in Texas. I guess his guilt obligated him to buy her the brand-new BMW in the driveway. With the luck she's having on her driving tests, she'll be ninety-three before she gets to drive it legally.

Erin jerks the car into park. "Get out, biatches."

"Aren't you so excited?" The girls giggle as we walk to the front door.

Excited—no. Nervous—yes. I strain a smile.

Jessica grabs my hand with enthusiasm. "This is a huge compliment, April! Not everyone gets this, you know."

"Yeah," Brianna agrees. "It took me way long to get invited to sign it."

"That's 'cause you were a skeez before you met us, Bri," Britney snaps as she keys her way into the house.

Every time I'm in Britney's room, I immediately think of a drag queen's dressing room. Not that I've ever seen a drag queen's dressing room . . . or even know what one would look like, for that matter. But I just assume that it might look like a glitter fairy threw up pink sparkles and sequins all over it. And that's exactly what Brit's room looks like—a pink glitter fairy's vomit factory.

"Don't just stand around, guys. You all have asses; use them!"

The four of us sit down halfway through her sentence. We've all developed quick reflexes in order to fulfill Brit's constant demands. I find myself sitting on the uncomfortable red high-heeled chair.

Britney skips to her dresser and pulls out the mysterious pink binder she scolded me about weeks ago. "Here it is, guys."

The girls clap. She removes a pink piece of paper from the three rings.

"Read it, Brit."

"Well, duh, Erin! What did you think I was going to do, eat it?" She walks over to me and clears her throat. "April, do you know what I'm holding right here?"

She doesn't give me time to answer.

"This is the *holy* Lipstick Oath. By signing it, you pledge your loyalty to the Lipstick Laws."

"What are the Lipstick Laws?" I ask cautiously.

"They're seven sacred laws that you have to follow if you want to be friends with us—or else!"

Or else? Or else what? Or else I'll be banished to Taiwan with only a raincoat and a piece of salami to survive? Oh, God. I'm doomed.

"You can only be invited to sign the Lipstick Oath when we think your popularity stock is high enough to benefit the group as a whole. You weren't ready when you tried to get your paws on this weeks ago," Britney says, swinging the paper. "You were a mess then. Really."

The girls shake their heads at me sympathetically. I'm embarrassed by their overtly condescending pity.

"But, other than a few fashion faux pas, you've cleaned up nicely since then," Britney adds. "And we think it's time now. Congratulations, April Bowers! This is your day!"

The girls clap and giggle while I hunch over with nerves on this hideous red chair.

"Thanks," I manage to gurgle out.

"Awww—she's so happy, she's speechless!" Jess sighs.

"Don't worry, April—I was the same way! It's like a dream, isn't it?" Brianna says.

I don't have time to respond before Britney persists with her well-rehearsed speech. "The Lipstick Laws cover the seven categories most important to our group." Her expression turns serious as she asks, "Are you ready for me to read them?"

Do I really have a choice in the matter? I nod in agreement.

"Lipstick Law One—Beauty. You are only as beautiful as your mirror tells you, so check it every hour."

I squint with bewilderment.

She elaborates. "It means never go an hour without checking your hair, makeup, clothes, and shoes. Head to toes!"

She rubs the length of her body up and down as if it's a prize on a game show.

"Okay," I say, thinking this is utterly ridiculous.

Britney adds, "You see, April, you may look great when you leave the house in the morning, but you could look like a scag three hours later . . . and wouldn't that be tragic?"

"I guess." I shrug.

She continues. "Lipstick Law Two—Fashion. Never sacrifice style for comfort."

"That means sweats are totally out," Jessica explains.

"That's *so* obvious, Jess! April isn't an idiot. Do you like insinuations that you're an idiot, April?"

"Umm . . ." I utter.

"That's what I thought," Britney says. "Anyhow, you need to work on this new fashion niche of yours."

After a few disastrous fashion Frankenstein flops (specifically one involving a plaid vest, a bedazzled rocker T-shirt, leggings, a head scarf, and platform shoes), Britney agreed that I should change my "pairer" fashion niche. I chose "casual chic" as my new niche, which is so much more me; I don't know why I didn't think of it to begin with . . . but Britney hasn't been too supportive of the idea.

"You need to focus more on the chic part rather than the casual part. You don't want to look like a hopeless homemaker. You'd be violating Lipstick Law Two. Got it?"

I nod my head in agreement, and she moves on. "Lipstick Law Three—Health. Never gain more than three pounds in a year."

"With the exception of PMS water bloat," Erin insists.

Brit looks up from the page in disgust. "No one gains three pounds of water bloat, unless you're an undercover heifer."

Erin's face flushes. I suddenly understand her constant battle with food temptations.

"Lipstick Law Four—Social. Never socialize with any creatures from the geek kingdom." Britney glares at me. "We'll make an exception for your nerd herder brother. It's unfortunate, but you can't totally ignore family."

"Er . . . thanks," I mumble.

"Lipstick Law Five—Secrets. Your personal information and top secrets are sole property of the group, and must be shared immediately upon signing the Lipstick Oath."

"You might as well tell us, 'cause we're gonna find out anyhow." Brianna sniggers.

The image of a Kleenex box—my deepest addiction—floats into my head. I almost choke on my own spit.

"Guys—God! This would go so much quicker if you shut the freak up and let me read!" Britney shouts, resuming her composure instantly. "This next one's the cardinal girl rule and should be a no-brainer . . . but, as we've found before, some girls have no brains."

Brianna laughs hysterically at this statement before Britney continues. "Lipstick Law Six—Love. All ex-boyfriends, current boyfriends, crushes, love interests, and flings are strictly off-limits to the rest of the group."

I immediately think of Mr. Hottie-Body Brentwood. It's taken me weeks to get his attention off of Britney and back on me. He's mine, and she'd better know it!

"And last, but definitely not least!" She raises her voice for added drama. "Lipstick Law Seven—General. Every individual decision must be made for the good of the group to benefit our popularity stock as a whole."

Is that it? Well, they're not asking too much . . . just for me to sign my life away, that's all. What have I gotten myself into?

"Do you have any questions?" Jessica asks eagerly.

"Well . . . so . . . you want me to check the mirror twenty-four/seven, put up with pain as long as it's fashionable, starve myself if I start to gain weight, ban all conversations with less popular people, share my deepest secrets—however embarrassing they may be, follow the cardinal girl rule by not associating with any past or present flames of others, and base all of my decisions solely on how they will affect the group?" I yap, completely out of breath by the end.

Impressed, Erin utters, "Whoa, you're a totally fast learner."

"That's why I like her so much, Erin. She's a jumbo-me. April, I couldn't have summed everything up better myself!" Britney professes proudly.

"Well"—I pause in thought—"what happens if I choose not to sign the Oath?"

Gasps of disbelief circulate the room like swarming mosquitoes.

"I mean, not that that's what I'm going to do," I say. "I'm just curious."

Erin gulps in shock. "That's never happened before—everyone signs the Lipstick Oath!"

"You'd be nuts not to sign it!" Brianna adds. "It's like the Academy Award of popularity—only the best are chosen!"

Looking at the girls suspiciously, I wonder . . . where are all the other Lipstick Law followers? They make it seem like hundreds have signed the Lipstick Oath and millions more are waiting to sign it. Yet there are only four of them here. I picture a mass Lipstick Law graveyard—with one lipstick gravestone that reads:

APRIL ELIZABETH BOWERS
LIVED TO THE GRAND AGE OF FIFTEEN.
SADLY, SHE WAS STARVED
BY LIPSTICK LAW THREE.

"I know girls who would *die* to sign the Lipstick Oath!" Jessica reveals, confirming my fear.

"What will happen if someone decides not to sign?" Britney repeats my question, looking appalled. "Well, we'd make sure that scag would be a social misfit for the rest of her skankful life."

Well then, that pretty much sums it up. I'm either doomed to follow their ridiculous Lipstick Laws, or I'll be condemned to misfit-dom for the rest of my life. I sit in silence, weighing my options.

The girls gather around me.

"Are you going to sign?" Britney inquires, holding up bright red lipstick. I have a sinking feeling that this is the lipstick Haley warned me about.

My heart races as I contemplate my doomed choices. I could either have a first-rate social life but be controlled by these crazy laws . . . or I could have Britney on my bad side, making sure I'm the laughingstock of Penford High School. I picture being tortured and laughed at through the halls. I picture Mr. Hottie-Body Brentwood running away from me in repulsive disgust . . . and . . . I give in. I just can't risk the alternative to the Lipstick Laws.

"Yeah, okay—I'll sign." I quickly apologize to Haley in my head. "So, what do you want me to do, sign my name in lipstick?"

"No, silly," Britney says. "First you have to pledge your loyalty. Put up your right hand."

Reluctantly, I follow her order and raise my right hand.

"Repeat after me: I, April Bowers."

"I—I . . . April Bowers," I choke out stiffly.

"Pledge my commitment to the Lipstick Laws and fellow members."

Feeling somewhat helpless, like a car stuck on the tracks of an oncoming train, I repeat it word for word: "Pledge my commitment to the Lipstick Laws and fellow members."

"I promise to follow all seven laws strictly, knowing that my popularity is dependent on my ability to fulfill them," Britney says slowly.

I repeat it all word for pathetic word, kicking myself with each syllable that escapes my lips.

She smiles, hands me the lipstick, and says, "Good! Now, put the lipstick on your lips and kiss the bottom of the paper—underneath the Lipstick Laws. Then we'll all do the same."

"It's like a blood oath, but with lipstick . . . same color, cuter idea," Erin says.

I smear the hideous blood-red lipstick over my lips and grab the paper in contempt. I don't want to go through with this, but with Britney's wicked eyes staring me into a coma, coupled with my fear of mass rejection at school, I bite the bullet and smooch the bottom of the paper. Yes, that's right; I kiss my rights away into the hands of a sadistic popularity nazi.

The girls follow my lead. One by one, their kisses join mine underneath Lipstick Laws One through Seven.

"Now, April, is there anything you want to tell us?" Britney says aggressively. "Remember, your secrets are our property now."

She taps her designer shoe on the dull hardwood floor. I immediately picture my manic bra-stuffing and thousands of innocent tissues being shoved into my boobicle cubicle bra cups. I begin to panic behind my frozen stare. To buy myself some time, I ask, "Wouldn't you guys like to share your secrets with me first?"

I smile and nod at them hopefully, thinking this is a perfectly normal request. They stare back at me in bafflement.

Britney rolls her eyes. "April, don't you get it? Sharing your dark secrets from before the Lipstick Laws is part of your initiation. We all had our initiations long ago."

"So, this is a one-way secret street today? Isn't that sort of unfair?" I say.

"Life isn't fair. It's not our fault that you're joining our group after us. You'll get to know our secrets over time, but it's your turn to fess up right now, not ours." Brit smirks.

"Make it good!" Erin adds, her muted blue eyes wide with anticipation.

My bottom lip quivers with dread. Oh my gosh . . . Haley was right. They *are* evil circus clowns, aren't they? I have to divulge something, because the bottom line is that I need friends . . . even if they're evil circus clown friends.

"Well?" the girls urge impatiently.

"Okay," I yelp out of frustration. "I have a secret."

But I just can't bring myself to tell them that I'm a bosom sculptor.

"I . . . errrrr . . . I like Matthew Brentwood!" I blurt out.

Britney sighs. "Please, April, that's not a secret."

"Tell us something juicy!" Brianna prods.

"Ummm . . . well . . . I kind of made up this name for him." I put my head down. "It's sort of stupid, though."

"Tell us! What is it?" they beg.

"It's ummm . . . Mr., errrr . . ."

"Mr. what?"

"Mr. Hottie-Body Brentwood," I divulge in sheer embarrassment.

Erin and Brianna burst into laughter.

"That's pathetic!" Erin derides.

Great, that's particularly compelling coming from a girl who could pass as a tall Oompa Loompa.

"How juvenile," Britney ridicules. "You shouldn't tell people that; it's totally embarrassing!"

No kidding. I mean, it's not like I was enthused about telling them or anything. They had to practically beat it out of me.

"What else, April? There has to be something else. Don't tell me we just inducted a boring chumpnut into our group." The look of disgrace on Britney's face is pressure enough.

"Okay, I have something else," I say, trying to impress her.

The girls creep in to me as if I'm going to reveal a huge, juicy scandal. I take a deep breath, wondering if I'll muster the courage to confess my true secret.

"I'm a . . . I'm . . ."

"You're a what?"

Ugh! I just can't do it! So, I say the first thing that pops into my mind that sounds halfway decent: "I'm a virgin!"

Britney shakes her head and laughs.

"April, April, April . . . What are we going to do with you? That's all you have to tell us? You're a *virgin?* No kidding? I woulda never guessed it," she says sarcastically. "Well, at least we know you're not a skeez. You could probably teach Brianna a thing or two."

I glance over at Brianna, who's grinding her teeth with spite.

"Hopefully you're not keeping anything from us. 'Cause we can kick you out at any time," Britney warns. "So, I'd strongly suggest that you follow all of the laws all of the time. If you do that, we'll be your BFFs."

"Best friends forever?" I ask, feeling relieved.

"No, April! Unconditional acceptance leads to letting yourself go. We'll be your best friends til you F up!" she barks.

Gulp. I feel my heart pounding out of my chest. Yes, it's a fact; I have sealed the deal. I stamped, certified, and lipsticked my life in a package sent through Priority Mail directly to the devil herself . . . and there's no turning back.

chapter six

Three and a half hours later, my mom is having a connip-
tion fit.

"Mom, I don't have a cell because you and Dad took it
away!" I argue. "That's why I couldn't call!"

"Oh—so this is my fault all of a sudden? You're telling
me it's my own fault that I thought my baby was taken by
a hooligan?"

"Aren't you being a tad dramatic?" I reason with her.

"Dramatic? Next, I suppose you'll tell me that Britney lives
in the backwoods and has no phones in her whole home. Do
you go to the bathroom in an outhouse there too?"

"No, Mom." I huff.

"And look at your face! Look at your lips! Since when do
you wear cheap, tacky bright red lipstick? It's like I don't even
know you anymore!" Her eyes become glossy. She grabs a few
tissues and blows her nose. I feel really bad for making her upset, but I also can't help but cringe at the fact that she's using up
my boob bud fillers.

"Mom, please . . . don't cry," I plead. "It's really not what
you think. It's not even my lipstick!"

"Just like it's not your fault that you didn't call, right?"

I see this is going nowhere. I need to make amends quickly
or my chances of sleeping over at Britney's tomorrow will
be zilch.

"No, you're right. It's my fault. I was going to call you when I got there and I just lost track of time. You're the one who wants me to make new friends, right?" I try to project some blame.

"Of course I want you to make friends! I want you to be happy—but I also want you to be responsible about it. That's not too much to ask, April. If your father knew about this, he'd have a ministroke!"

Tad dramatic again . . . but I pretend to agree. "I know, Mom, I'm so sorry. It will never happen again. I promise."

"I love you, sweetheart, and I don't want anything bad to happen to you," she mutters as she squeezes me so hard, my ribs almost crack.

Oh, Lord, if she only knew the trouble I got myself into signing the Lipstick Oath. I decide not to tell her about it. I just smile and reply, "I know, Mom. I love you too."

That same night I wake from another horrible nightmare. I dream that I'm standing on a large stage in the middle of the school gymnasium. A big, bright spotlight is pointing directly at me. I flinch, trying to cover my eyes from the blinding glare. Britney Taylor hops onto the stage wearing an elaborate circus ringleader outfit. She's followed by Brianna, Erin, and Jessica, who are dressed as evil clowns and juggling lipstick. Britney has a whip and a megaphone, and she begins to yell, "Step right up, step right up! Behold the human tissue box! Call her a freak of nature, a useless spectacle, or my lipstick slave. Call her what you must, but just know that I own her!"

A crowd forms around the stage, chanting, "Human tissue box! Lipstick slave! Human tissue box! Lipstick slave!"

Britney walks up to me with her whip. She smears blood-red lipstick all over my face. And then, one by one, she proceeds to pull out 110 tissues from my sagging bra.

It takes me a while to fall back to sleep after the night terror. I finally doze off with both hands protecting my sesame seed chest.

My mom drops me off at five p.m. on Saturday.

Britney erupts as she opens the door, "April, where on earth have you been?"

She grabs my arm and drags me into the house like a blond tow truck.

"I-I'm on time . . . Right?" I stammer.

"Yeah—but we've been trying to call you for like the last hour to come early. Oops . . . I forgot, though . . . someone's stuck in the 1900s without a cell phone," she gripes as I follow her up the narrow stairs.

"Sorry, I went to the mall with my mom. What's going on?"

"Kyle Smith and Hilary Snyder broke up."

"Oh?" I say, not understanding how this affects me.

Britney rolls her eyes at my naiveté and says, "When the senior quarterback becomes single, you have to jump on him like a free cruise to Maui. We're supposed to be at his house in ten minutes. So, you have like three seconds to get your swim-suit on."

Whoa . . . whoa . . . wait a second . . . Did she just say swim-suit? Is she crazy? Holy crap, not only will my tissue boobs sop up all the water in a pool, it's fifty-four degrees outside and I didn't pack a suit.

As if she's reading my thoughts, she says, "Don't worry, it's an indoor pool."

"Ummm . . . I didn't pack a swimsuit. I didn't know," I utter, wishing my mother was still in the driveway so I could run back to her car for a quick escape.

"I've got you covered; I have tons of suits. Erin had to borrow one too. Too bad she looks like a stuffed sausage in it," she announces as she opens the door to her gaudy bedroom.

"What?" Erin cries, sitting on the unsightly high-heeled chair, looking as if her life dreams have been smashed to a pulp. I shake my head, passing an empathetic expression to her.

Standing among a pile of at least twenty-five bathing suits in Britney's bathroom, I find myself praying to God: "Dear God, please let this be a dream . . . and if, for some cruel and senseless reason, this isn't a dream, but an actual living night-mare . . . please let there be a minor earthquake at Kyle Smith's home that drains all the water from his pool before we get there. Amen."

"Hurry up, April!" the girls yell on the other side of the door.

Impatient jerks! I try on a bikini top over my stuffed bra. This clearly isn't going to work. After all, I have to leave my bra on. I have nothing to hold up my Kleenex bosom without it. God knows my real woman-sprouts aren't budded enough to hold anything up. I'll have to choose a less trendy, more functional one-piece.

"Black is flattering," I whisper to myself as I slide on a one-piece halter. I slip my bra straps off my shoulders and tuck them into the boobicle cubicle cups. I hope no one will be able to tell that I have my bra on with about forty-five tissues securely stuffed into both sides underneath Britney's suit.

"A one-piece? You're like the Virgin Mary, April!" Britney heckles as I emerge from the bathroom. If only that were the case. Carrying the next Messiah would be the least of my problems at this point.

"What's that?" Jessica points to my back.

Oh, no! This is it! I'm done for! I'm caught red-handed. My secret world of bosom sculpting is crashing down around me. I'm destined for bra-stuffing rehab in a distant boobicus minimus land, I just know it.

Britney laughs. "I wouldn't be caught dead in that thing. That's why the tag's still on it."

Oh, thank you, God; they're talking about the sales tag. Now, just please create that earthquake we discussed a minute ago . . .

"Hang on, April, I'll get it off," Britney says, walking toward me with scissors. She shakes her head. "You know you should never wear a one-piece unless you're a lard ass or over thirty, right?"

"Sorry," I say bashfully, looking at the ground as she cuts the tag off. I really want to ask her why she has one-pieces to choose from if they're such an atrocity. Unfortunately, I don't have the nerve to ask.

The car ride to Kyle's house is totally uncomfortable for many reasons, among them the following:

- Erin is driving like a bat out of hell, still jacked about the stuffed sausage comment.
- I tied the halter too tightly around my neck . . . and I can barely feel anything below my shoulders.
- Jess and Brianna are fighting over whose wrists are skinnier, and I'm in the middle of them.
  And . . .
- I'm trying desperately to come up with an excuse not to swim.

The Smiths are local celebrities because of their big New York State Lottery win five years ago. Their house is sickening, it's so big. Gorgeous Kyle Smith is waiting for us outside. He leads us into the dreaded pool house. I'm too scared to check him out because of Lipstick Law Six. I don't even dare make eye contact with him. I know Britney has the hots for him, and any communication—including nonverbal—is a definite Lipstick Law no-no.

I wrap a beach towel around my shoulders like a shawl and sit by the edge of the Olympic-size indoor pool. While the others splash and laugh in the water, I'm determined to sit on the deck like an unmovable cement statue.

"Come in, April," Jessica pleads.

"That's okay. I can't swim, but I'm having fun watching you." Total lie, but a good one. It sounds like a logical excuse. They wouldn't want to see me oink to the bottom like a bowling ball . . . or maybe they would. My paranoia takes hold.

I'm pretty sure that Britney hasn't even noticed that I'm not in the pool. She should really learn how to play hard to get. Doesn't she know that guys like a challenge? Her incessant flirting with Kyle makes me want to hurl, but at least it keeps her distracted.

A short, chubby boy who resembles a slug with arms and legs comes sauntering in. He has way too much body hair to be a teenager. On the contrary, I'm sure I recognize him from school.

"What's this? A party, and I wasn't invited? What's the explanation?" His crackly voice could make a pig squeal.

"Come in, Brandon. The water is warm, and the ladies are hot!" Kyle says, smiling at Britney. She sucks up the flattery like a straw.

Ick. I know who slug boy is . . . Brandon Smith—the popular junior who's only popular because of his brother. Everyone knows one of those kids—not a prize to look at or talk to . . . but the random coincidence of having a gorgeous, athletic older brother vaults the younger sibling into popularity through no effort of his own.

"Cannonball!" the large oaf shouts as he flings himself off the side of the pool in an upright fetal position.

I quickly move out of the way, but my fast reflexes aren't enough. I'm soaked. Luckily, the towel covering my chest area has protected my tissues from the damage that could have been done by the flooding.

Dear God, I pray, *Thank you for the earthquake. Although I didn't mean for it to be caused by a showoff performing a cannonball, I appreciate the effort. Amen.*

"Why's a pretty lady like you sitting like a wallflower?"

Shoot, Brandon has spotted me.

"I can't swim," I explain.

"Everyone can swim. How hard is it? You just do this." He flails his arms vigorously.

"I assure you, if I did that, I'd drown," I say, thoroughly unimpressed.

"Oh, yeah? Would you really?" he mocks.

It's at this very moment that my whole life and bra-stuffing addiction flash before my eyes. He grabs my legs like a tug-of-war rope and pulls me into the deep end of the pool. Water goes up my nose, my tissues are engulfed by liquid, and I immediately pop to the top of the pool with a bloodcurdling scream. I pull myself up on the deck and speed like a demon to the pool house bathroom. Everything happens so fast: if it hadn't been for my death screech, I'm sure no one would've even noticed.

"I thought you couldn't swim!" Bandon yells behind me.

I sit in the huge wood-paneled bathroom for a good while, panicking, crying, and trying to come up with a plausible solution for my lumpy, soggy problem that was once my voluptuous fake boobage. I quickly scoop the mess out from my chest and dump the drenched tissues in the toilet. The weight of all the sponged-up water makes enormous *plop* sounds as if I'm taking a gigantic poo.

"I hope no one can hear this," I whisper to myself.

Knock, knock, knock—Jessica and Brandon pound on the door.

"You okay in there?"

"No, I'm not! No thanks to Brandon!" I reply.

"Sorry, April. I didn't know."

Yes, he did. I grimace. I told him I can't swim. Sure, it's a lie, but he doesn't know that.

I look at my flat bare chest against the shiny black spandex of the suit in the mirror. What am I going to do? My clothes are in the other room. I'll have to walk out at some point to get them. Oh—please go away, guys . . . so I can sneak out.

"We're not going to leave until we know you're okay," Jess says.

"I'm okay!" I whimper.

"It doesn't sound like it. Sounds like you're taking a massive dump!" Brandon so pleasantly announces.

"It seems like you could swim all right. So what's the matter?" Jessica asks.

"I'm fine, guys. I'm just allergic to chlorine," I say brilliantly on the spur of the moment.

"Oh my gosh! Do you need a doctor?" Jess panics.

"No! Oh—no . . . Please . . . I'll be okay . . . I'm just sorta sick right now."

"April, I'm staying right here. You say the word, and I'll call 911."

Yes, sure, that's all I need . . . the paramedics to come and find a perfectly healthy girl who has locked herself in the bathroom, completely hysterical over the remnants of her spongy chestoid tissues in the toilet. That would be a sure ticket to the loony bin, if you ask me.

"What's wrong with her?" Brianna and Erin squeal outside the door.

Great, this is becoming a huge freak show.

"She's sick, diarrhea," Brandon whispers, loud enough for me to hear.

"Guys, I'm fine. I'll be okay. Go back in the pool."

I have to think quick on my feet. They aren't leaving, and they're becoming more persistent by the second. I quickly glance down . . . and bingo. That's when I see it—a roll of nice, dry toilet paper. I begin unraveling it in heaps and stuffing it into the top of the suit. Yeah, it's soaking up some of the water from the bathing suit, but it's holding up pretty well. It will definitely be good enough for me to walk out to get my sweater and jeans.

I emerge from the bathroom five minutes later, completely embarrassed and thinking my social life is over.

"Took you long enough. Are you okay?" the girls ask, following me into the other room, where my clothes are hanging innocently in a closet.

"I just need to get dressed," I say, shooing them out of the changing room. "Privacy, please!"

"Damn, she used all the toilet paper and clogged the pot! Funny thing is, her shit doesn't even stink!" I hear Inspector Brandon yelling from the bathroom.

⁓⊙⊱⁓

"Thanks for almost drowning, April. It gave me some alone time with Kyle," Britney says with a devious grin. "He's an amazing kisser."

We're finally back at her house. I've changed into my pajamas and am trying to erase the trauma of the night from my mind.

Jessica comes closer, inspecting me for death bumps. "Why didn't you tell us you're allergic to chlorine?"

"Well, I know what good friends you are . . . and I felt like if I had told you, you might've canceled your plans. I didn't want to ruin your fun," I say, trying to make them feel guilty.

It's unsuccessful.

"We wouldn't have canceled," Britney says impatiently. "Don't act like some saint, April. I'm allergic to peanuts, but I wouldn't ban everyone else from throwing a peanut butter party. Anyhow, considering the geek procedure you pulled, I can't believe that Brandon thinks you're hot. I mean, you looked like a total nerd-herding chumpnut tonight."

"What?" Erin, Brianna, and Jess blurt simultaneously, as if they're sharing the same brain.

"I'd rather not know," I mutter under my breath.

"Yeah, Brandon totally digs April. He even asked if we want to go to Troy Hoffman's annual bonfire in two weeks. Yummo! What I wouldn't do to get with Troy. If only I could find a way to bump off his girlfriend," she says casually, picking at her fingernail polish.

"April, did you hear that? Brandon invited you to Troy's bonfire party! You're so lucky! He digs you, and he's totally popular," Jessica recaps.

Getting invited to Troy's party is a big deal; he's the most coveted guy in Penford High School. But getting invited to accompany Brandon the slug makes me want to vomit.

"Ummmm . . . no, I'm not going," I state matter-of-factly.

"Ummm . . . yes, you are!" Britney argues.

I throw up a little in my mouth. "Brit, I think he's beyond repulsive!"

"It doesn't matter what you think. According to Lipstick Law Seven, your decision is based on the group as a whole.

Brandon is totally popular—and you're totally going!" she demands.

"I don't even know if I'll be available," I reason.

"Oh, yeah, like you have other plans. What, with your dork-tower brother? If you're not already available, you'll make yourself available!" She twists her lips into a scowl.

I loathe her. Unfortunately, I lipsticked my soul to the twit.

"But you know I like Matt, and I'll ruin things with him if I go out with someone else," I say.

"Boo-hoo! The sacrifices you have to make for friends . . ." Britney says, antagonizing me with a fake smile.

I temporarily pause at the word *friends*. She's right: If I screw this up, I may not have any friends at all. But, on the other hand, friends should want what's best for me, right? And, clearly, Brandon is not what's best for me!

"Brit, I can't—"

"You're not even dating Matt! Come to think of it, you haven't even talked to him on the phone, have you?"

I look down with embarrassment. It is pretty pathetic now that she says it like that. I don't have a cell, and I don't want to give him my home number. I mean, I can't risk my brother answering the phone and humiliating me.

"You have to get over him!" Britney points her finger at me heatedly. "I've liked Kyle since the sixth grade, and since I can't have Troy as long as he's with that skanky girlfriend, Kyle will have to do. And you're not going to ruin my chances with him!

"Since Kyle and Brandon are brothers, and Brandon likes you, you'll have to pretend to like him as long as I need you to. That means you can't talk to Matt until I say so! Or else, you'll be violating your Lipstick Oath."

Enough with the Lipstick Laws already! I feel like strangling Brat-ney!

"Anyway," Erin says to antagonize me, "you know Brandon is going to kiss you, right?"

I raise my voice. "No way. I can assure you I will not be kissing Brandon Smith ever!"

Jessica tries to calm me. "You'll be fine, April. There'll be so many people at the bonfire, you guys might not even be alone to make out."

"Remember Emma last year?" Brianna recalls hauntingly. "He totally harassed her, and now she's at a private boarding school."

"I heard she has a lip ring and wears black lipstick now, too. What a freak funnel." Britney laughs.

"What happened?" I yelp in fear, suddenly forgetting how mad I am.

"They went on a date last year, and not only did he say she's the sloppiest, most disgusting kisser . . . he pulled tube socks out of her bra!" Britney cackles.

The other girls burst into laughter.

"Can you imagine? Someone actually thinking that she can get away with stuffing tube socks in her bra?" Erin says. "Pathetic!"

I glance down at my toilet-paper-padded chest and tremble in terror. The horrifying thought of Brandon the slug releasing tissues from my bra like caged doves keeps me up all night.

chapter seven

I'm in so much pain, I can barely breathe. My feet are throbbing, and I have no idea how I'm going to get through the night. I don't care if these horrendous lime green torture chambers are from a Paris fashion show. They are hideous, and they hurt! At this point, I'd rather be wearing swimming flippers or clown stilts than what Britney made me change into.

"Remember Lipstick Law Two, April. Shame on you," Brit scolded earlier this evening. Apparently, she didn't approve of my original shoe choice. "Here, put these on."

"But Brit . . . these are a size six and a half. I'm a size seven and a half."

"So? Never sacrifice style for comfort. Put them on!"

Britney never loses an argument. She's also the reason I'm not wearing a coat on my way to an outside party in November.

"You look like the Pillsbury Doughboy in that. You can't wear it!" she ordered.

So now I'm miserable and on my way to Troy Hoffman's party, with the head Lipstick Lawlord in front of me, tourniquet shoes below me, and slug boy of the year beside me. Brandon leans closer to me. His onion breath accosts my neck, making me nauseous.

"Don't be a stranger, April."

I'm not moving closer to him. I don't care what he says. I'm jammed as close to the back door of Kyle's Range Rover as I can be. I don't acknowledge him. I can't get Matt out of my mind. How did Britney convince me not to talk to him for two whole weeks? She's such a brainwasher! How will I ever explain ignoring him for Brandon the slug? Matt is going to forget about me. He probably already has.

Kyle parks among a sea of cars. Troy lives on several acres, and I'm sure that every bit of his parents' property will be torn to shreds from tire marks.

"Dude, you may never get out of here if the cops come," Brandon says. "Cars are gonna pile up behind you."

"Don't jinx us, bro," Kyle replies. "He lives in the middle of nowhere. Who's gonna call the cops?"

Actually, he doesn't live in the middle of nowhere. I know exactly where I am. My neighborhood is only about a mile up the road, which is good to know if I need to escape from Brandon's clutch.

"Is Jamie Bradshaw going to be here?" Britney asks as we get out of the SUV.

"Of course, she's Troy's girl," Kyle responds, putting his arm around her tiny waist.

Britney doesn't show it, but I know she's upset. She hates Jamie Bradshaw. She and Brit have been rivals for years. Jamie is the beautiful senior captain of the varsity cheerleading team. Britney insists that Jamie is the only reason she didn't make the team this year. "She's jealous of me" is her excuse. The truth is that Britney's eyes practically pop out of her head with envy every time Jamie is around. Jamie has the two things that Britney wants and can't have: a great personality, and more important, Troy Hoffman.

I limp through the fallen leaves, trying to keep up with Britney. I look like a ninety-year-old woman hobbling in these awful shoes. It's freezing outside, and I'm shivering like crazy. Brandon places his jacket over my shoulders. It smells like a Mexican restaurant. I'm reminded of how much I dislike Mexican food.

"Thanks, Brandon," I say, breathing in and out through my mouth, trying to spare my nose the enchilada odor. Normally I'd be impressed with this act of chivalry. However, I know that Brandon is just trying to get some action tonight. Boy, is he going to be disappointed.

As we make our way to the bonfire in Troy's backyard, the air gets warm and thick with smoke. The crackling embers drown among the rowdy group of people. The obscene smell of marijuana marinates the atmosphere from a few yards away. A couple of useless stoners are having a powwow behind a patch of bushes. They're probably discussing their less-than-genius philosophies on life and the common cure for a mammoth munchie attack.

Kyle runs up to tackle a group of football players standing near a woodpile next to the house. He's greeted with loud cheers and a few "bro" punches. Warmer now that I'm next to the fire, I quickly give Brandon's enchilada jacket back and have a seat next to Britney on a log.

"Do you girls want a drink?" Brandon accommodates, still praying for a hookup, I'm sure.

"Of course." Britney smiles.

"Sure. I'll take a Diet Coke if they have it."

Brit nudges my ribs. Evidently that was the wrong answer.

"Right," Brandon replies sarcastically. He waddles into the house.

"He's so hot!" Britney whispers to me.

"Who? Brandon?" I gag.

"No!" She points to the group near the woodpile.

"Oh, yeah . . . Kyle is pretty hot," I agree.

"No! Not Kyle, him!" She points directly at Troy Hoffman, who's sipping a cold beer looking hotter than the bonfire. "Trust me, someday I'll get him away from that cow."

She shoots a dirty look across the bonfire at Jamie. Jamie doesn't notice. She's in the middle of telling a group of seniors an animated story. Her arms are flapping, and the group is laughing hysterically. I look at Brit with a smirk, reveling in her jealousy.

"This is lame," she says under her breath.

Her attitude instantly changes when Kyle returns. He asks her to go inside with him, and she quickly agrees.

"Hold my coat," she barks at me.

I'm sitting by myself. I don't know anyone here, and the only person who makes an attempt to talk to me is Pedro, a foreign exchange student who's completely saturated in Old Spice cologne.

"Your shoes, *me gusta!* Me like!" he says in broken English, staring at their hideousness.

"Thanks. They're really painful!" I explain with a friendly smile.

He grins and says, "Me wants to—to—" I lean closer, ready to help him translate as he tries to think of the right words. "Get . . ."

"A drink?" I try to help him.

"No," he continues. "Me wants to—to—get . . ."

He points to my jeans. My heart goes out to him. I can imagine how difficult it must be to be in a foreign country without a full grasp of the language.

"A pair of jeans? *Pantalones?*" I ask, trying to speak some Spanish.

"No, no!" Frustrated, he points again.

"What? You wanna sit here?" I pat the log next to me, happy to take him under my English-speaking wing.

"No . . . No . . . Me wants—to—to—get in . . ."

I lean even closer. "In what?"

"Your panties!" he blurts knowingly.

My mouth drops open in horror. I'm shocked.

"*Sí?*" He smirks.

"No! No panties!" I yell, completely disgusted.

Darren, an obnoxiously raucous senior, stumbles up to us.

"*Sí* . . . me-wantsta-get-inyur-panties tooooo! Noooo deal?" he slurs, spilling half of his beer down my shirt. It slowly seeps into my tissues.

"Told ya she'd fall for it, dude," Pedro says with a faint accent in near perfect English. "Me-me-wants-to-to . . ." he recaps his stammering antics, and bursts into laughter with Darren.

"Goooodjob, PED . . . RO . . . MY mannnn." Darren pats him on the back and hands him five dollars.

Humiliated, I wipe my shirt off, realizing I was part of a bet. Pedro obviously knew what he was doing all along. This just goes to show that regardless of the country they come from, all guys are pigs! I feel like oinking at them. Instead, I give them a withering look before stalking off.

I walk far away from the bonfire and find a secluded lawn chair to sit on. I'm freezing again, so I slip on Britney's expensive coat, making sure no beer rubs off on it. I can't believe that I'm actually wondering where Brandon is at this point.

Another fifteen minutes go by, and Brandon finally comes out with drinks.

"Why are you all the way over here? Where's Britney?" he asks.

"Kyle took her inside a while ago. I thought you would see them," I say curtly, deciding not to tell him about Pedro and Darren the perverts.

"They probably went upstairs." Brandon smiles sneakily. "I mixed you up something extra special. You can have Brit's, too."

He hands me a big mug. I take a whiff of the cocktail and practically fall off the chair. It smells like nail polish remover.

"Where did Troy get all this alcohol?" I ask, looking around at the crowd of hammered faces.

"Travis came home from college this weekend," Brandon replies.

Troy's brother—that makes sense. Travis Hoffman graduated years before I moved here, but even I know about him. It took him five years to graduate from high school . . . and he's going on his sixth year of college. He's definitely not there for the education.

"What's wrong?" Brandon notices the misery on my face.

"I'm . . ." Oh, no, I feel it. My annoyance cork is about to pop. I decide to let it all out. "I'm freezing, I want to saw my feet off, I've been sitting outside by myself for nine years . . . and I have beer down my shirt!"

"I can help you with that."

I smack his hand away from my chest. "Don't even think about it!"

"Well, sor-ry!" He backs up with his hands in the air. "You seem like you wanna get outta here."

"Is that an option?" I ask hopefully.

"Sure, we can go if you want." He smiles, dangling a set of car keys. "Kyle gave me his keys."

"Have you had anything to drink?" I look at him suspiciously.

"Negative." He shakes his head. "I'm on driving duty tonight."

"You think Brit will get mad at me? Will you come back for them later? I wouldn't want her to think I left her."

"Nah, she won't get mad. They won't even know we left. I'll come right back after I drop you off," he says convincingly.

I accept his offer and begin to hobble with him to Kyle's truck. I'm so cold, I decide to sip the gross drink he gave me. It tastes horrible, but at least it's warming me up. As we approach the SUV, we both realize that no less than ten cars have blocked us in since we first arrived.

"Great, we're going to be here all night," I grumble.

"That's not such a bad thing, is it? We can find plenty of things to do to pass the time." Brandon winks.

My stomach bubbles with revulsion. I begin to sip my drink faster to try to soothe it.

"Let's get in the car and turn on the heat. We can at least warm up a little."

His suggestion seems halfway plausible, since my teeth are chattering from the cold night breeze. I open the door and hop into the front seat with my booze mug.

Before I know it, I've finished my first drink, and Brandon replaces it with Britney's. I find that it's easier to look at his face the more I drink. Funny thing is, I don't even like alcohol. In fact, the only other time I've ever tried it was when Haley and I stole a couple of beers from my dad's beer fridge this past summer. We thought it would be fun to give her a bon voyage toast over a couple of brews. We took one sip of the beer and spit it out all over my bedroom. It was putrid! I practically peed my pants laughing that night.

Obviously, since I'm not an experienced drinker, the alcohol hits me pretty quickly. My body becomes warm and tingly and I can no longer feel my feet . . . Probably a combination of the alcohol and the tourniquet shoes. It's a super-weird sensation, but at least they don't hurt anymore.

"Is it hot in here now?" I ask, fanning my face with my hand.

"You're making it hot," he says suavely, turning down the car heat.

Brandon starts telling jokes, which I'm finding hilariously funny . . . not because of what he's saying, or how he's telling them . . . but because I've zoned in on one thick overgrown über-long black hair that's flopping from his chin as he talks. I immediately think of the Three Little Pigs . . . and how funny it would be if he were to lean in for a kiss and I were to say, "Not by the hair of your chinny-chin-chin." This thought, of course, is completely amusing to me until he actually moves closer.

"Let's face it, April," he says, "we've been checking each other out all night."

He brushes a few lingering curls away from my face and leans in even closer.

"Uh . . . no, I haven't," I challenge him.

"Don't try to play hard to get; I know you want to kiss me." He clasps my neck gently, pulling my face in to his.

"I don't think this is a good idea!" I blurt.

He puts his stumpy finger up to my mouth. "Shhhh . . . give in to temptation . . ."

I see his lips parting. I instantly think of poor Emma and her tube socks and get sick to my stomach. He's coming in closer . . . and closer . . . My eyes are bulging in fear as he's about to touch my lips with his crusty trout-suckers . . . when all of a sudden, my stomach lets out a huge *gurgle . . . blurp . . . gurgle . . . burble . . . glurp! Glurp!*

He pulls back.

"What was that?" He looks at me with repulsion.

"I don't feel so good," I say as I stumble out of the car to puke by the front tire.

He hops out quickly.

"Oh, shit!" he shouts.

"No, no . . . it's okay . . . I'm okay," I say, holding my hand up. Then I realize that he's not worried about me.

A bright light is shining toward us, and he screams, "COPS! RUUUUN!"

I dart so fast, you'd think a propeller is attached to my booty. It's hard to run when you can't feel your feet, but I manage, like a crazed convict on the loose. I surge through pricker bushes without even flinching. Soon I find myself wading in a swamp. Okay, maybe it's just a mud puddle, but regardless, it's wet. I quickly look back at the party scene. Kids are scattering everywhere, like a horde of ants dashing from an anteater. This encourages me to continue trucking it.

By the time I'm nearing home, the glow of a streetlamp lights my path. I realize that Britney's chic, expensive green shoes (although they're still hideous) are no longer green.

I remember her warning from earlier: "If anything happens to these, I'll *kill* you!"

I stop by a large tree to throw up again.

chapter eight

"Hi, Brit. It's me again. I'm just calling to see if you're okay. I haven't heard from you, and I'm worried. I'm so sorry about last night . . . and the cops . . . and everything. Please call me back as soon as you get this!"

This is the eighth message I've left on Britney's cell. She isn't returning my calls, which can't be a good sign.

It was hard, but I managed to get the prickers and burrs out of her jacket. Unfortunately, now it looks like a cat's scratching post. Also, scrubbing her shoes in my bathroom sink wasn't the brightest idea. I don't think the fabric's washable. I pace my room obsessively with a monstrous headache. I'm terrified for Monday . . . and I should be.

"It's okay. It'll be fine. I'll just pay her back for the shoes and coat." I try to console myself. "There was nothing I could do. I couldn't help it. She has to understand."

"I am going to KILL YOU!" Britney screams after I hand over her ruined coat and shoes. "Don't even look at me! Don't talk to me! You're *dead* in my world!"

She throws them back at me with a venomous look in her eyes. Her once green shoes miss my head by a centimeter.

"I'm sorry! I'll pay you back!"

She stomps up to me. I'm afraid she's going to bite my nose off because she's so close to my face. "You're dead, April! Dead girls don't talk! So, shut it!"

I gather my gym clothes and run to the bathroom. My chin trembles as I lock the door. Sobbing, I panic—oh my gosh, she's going to ruin my life! It's bad enough that Matt refused to talk to me in homeroom and the whole football team is calling me "Pukie." But more than anything, I'm terrified of what Britney is going to do to me . . . if she doesn't decide to kill me first.

A couple minutes after the first-period bell rings, I pull myself together as best as I can and walk into the gymnasium. I'm pretty sure makeup is streaming down my face. I don't know . . . I didn't look in the mirror, a clear violation of Lipstick Law One.

"Just give her time to cool down. She's just mad. She'll get over it eventually. You'll pay her back." I talk quietly to myself like a crazy person. "Just give her space for now. Keep your distance."

"Ms. Hoops!" Britney yells from the opposite side of the gymnasium.

"Yes, Miss Taylor?" the gym teacher responds.

"I need a new gym partner!"

"Oh, no, I can't do that. If you're having problems, you need to work them out with your partner. That's an important part of becoming an adult, Britney," she explains.

Britney stamps her foot childishly. "But, but . . . our problems can't be resolved!" she insists, pointing at me.

Ms. Hoops grows concerned. "What on earth is wrong, Britney?"

"April . . . April has foot fungus!"

I gasp. "Liar! What are you talking about?"

"Don't pretend like you don't, April! Admit it: you have mushrooms growing from your toes!" Britney says as the other students laugh.

I cross my arms defiantly and repeat, "Liar!"

"Britney, foot fungus is no reason to switch partners," Ms. Hoops says calmly. "April can get something to take care of that."

"But I don't—" I blurt before Britney's loud voice overtakes mine.

"Well, nothing is going to cure her herpes! That's incurable!"

"What? I don't have *herpes!*" I shout adamantly. I want to rip her hair out!

"Don't pretend like you didn't try to give me your herpes on the first day of school when you gave me your lip gloss!" Britney's head jerks as she yells; her long ponytail bounces viciously behind her.

Ms. Hoops takes us out into the hall. It's too late, though. They all think I have herpes and foot fungus now. I want to kill Britney. After fifteen minutes of unresolved screaming with Ms. Hoopensteiner trying to calm us down, she decides to pair us with new partners.

Nancy Herman, my new gym partner and locker neighbor, puts her hand on my shoulder and whispers, "Don't worry, April. I have foot fungus too."

Avoiding Britney as much as possible, I skip the cafeteria fifth period. My stomach is a mess. I wouldn't be able to eat anything, anyway. Not to mention, I know Mr. Hottie-Body

Brentwood is angry with me, too. He has every right to be. I ignored him for a troll man with a black chin hair the size of a long fishing line. Why wouldn't he be angry? I'm mad at myself!

I'm sitting at a cubby in the library, looking out at the courtyard. King Stalker McGerk of Loserhood is three cubbies away, appearing completely overjoyed by my presence. I try not to acknowledge that I feel his radar eyes sizing me up. Instead, I wonder if my life will ever be the same. How could things have gone so wrong? Hopefully I can clear things up with Jessica next period. She's the most reasonable of them all.

I walk into Señor Gonzales's Spanish class sixth period, immediately noticing that Jessica's desk is empty. That's not like her; she's usually here early.

The class fills and she's still missing. I pray that I get the chance to talk to her. She can't deny me to my face, right? The bell rings, and she scoots in as the teacher closes the door. A big whiff of her flowery perfume breezes by when she sits down next to me. As the teacher begins his lecture, I stare over at her, hoping she'll look at me. She doesn't.

"Pssst . . . Jess . . ." I whisper.

She ignores me.

"Jess . . ." I say a little louder.

Still ignores me.

"Jessica!" I say a bit too loudly.

Señor Gonzales points at me. "Señorita Abril, *silencio, por favor!*"

"Sorry," I say. "I mean, *lo siento.*"

I wait until he leaves the room to make copies before trying to talk to her again.

"Jessica, please talk to me."

"I can't, April. What you did is pretty messed up!" she snaps.

"I didn't mean to ruin Britney's stuff! It was an accident! I told her I'd pay her for it. So, what did I do that was so bad?"

"Ummm . . . well, duh, you're the reason twenty-five of our classmates got underage drinking citations . . . and Travis Hoffman is sitting in the county jail for purchasing alcohol for minors." She rolls her eyes at me.

"What?" I shout. Everyone turns to look at me. "I didn't call the cops!"

"That's not what Britney says. She has a voice mail to prove it. You're apologizing about the cops on it. She said you were probably getting back at her for making you go with Brandon. Not too smart."

That little blond witch twisted my words! I scowl just thinking about it. "Seriously, Jessica, would I be stupid enough to call the cops on a party that I was at? I don't even have a cell phone, remember? How would I have called? Go ask Brandon; he was with me!"

The teacher comes back in. I face forward, still fuming. Jess quickly whispers, "I don't know, April. You just need to talk it over with Brit."

A few periods later, I'm shocked to see Britney and Erin waiting for me outside of Mr. Stuart's history class. This is it. This is where I am going to die.

I try to talk to them. "You know I didn't call the—"

"Shut it, April!" Britney grabs my bag and pulls me into the girls' bathroom across the hall. I cover my face with my hand, thinking she's going to hit me.

"You're coming with us," she orders. "We need to talk."

Talk? I'm all about talking. As long as it doesn't involve hitting or spitting . . . or telling people that I have herpes and foot fungus.

"Yeah," I agree. "We do need to talk. I'll go anywhere you want after school."

"No, we need to talk now!" she demands.

I realize she wants me to skip class.

"But," I say nervously, "Mr. Stuart—"

"What, are you scared?" Brit taunts. "Suck it up; we're skipping class, too."

Yeah, but they both have study hall with Mr. Bilsby this period. And everyone knows he can barely see over his own nose to worry about attendance. That's a lot different than having class with Satan's bodyguard. Their eyes narrow at me as I contemplate what it will feel like when Mr. Stuart puts me through a meat grinder for skipping his class.

"Do you care more about Mr. Stuart being mad at you or us hating you forever?" Erin asks.

"Well, you guys hating me," I admit.

"Then let's go," they say.

I follow them hopelessly to the red car. Erin turns the music up so loud, I can't hear myself think. She speeds out of the parking lot. Images of Mr. Stuart peeling my skin like a tangerine creep into my mind.

"Where are we going?" I ask timidly. Either they can't hear me over the music or they're ignoring me on purpose. I begin to recognize the area. My stomach turns to mush as Erin parks in a field across from Troy Hoffman's property.

"Look familiar?" Britney says.

"I—"

"I came here to talk to you . . . not to hear you talk to me!" she snaps.

Erin smiles, soaking up the drama like a mop.

"Thanks to you," Britney says sarcastically, "there will now be a Lipstick Law Eight. Do you know what it's going to be, April?"

I shake my head no, trying not to cry.

"Lipstick Law Eight—never ditch your friends at a party!" she screams.

"But . . . I didn't—"

"Shut it, April!" Brit turns around to point at my face. "I had to hide from the cops in a dirty laundry bin because of you! I'm probably gonna get scabies or salmonella!"

"You ditched me to go inside with Kyle!" I rebut.

"Don't you dare try to blame this on me! Regardless, you broke the Lipstick Laws! Do you know what that means?" She sneers, not giving me time to answer. "It means you're out of our group! You're done. Cooked. The end. Sayonara. The fat lady's sung."

"But . . . how did I break the laws? Which laws did I break?" I cry out.

"I'm hurt, April," she says. "You don't even know what you did? Hmm . . ." Britney pauses, tapping her long fingernail on her chin sarcastically. "Well, let me inform you. First, you broke Lipstick Law Two by not respecting fashion. You *ruined* my precious stuff! So, you pretty much flushed our fashion law right down the toilet with your reputation!"

"I told you I'd pay you back," I say quickly.

"They were one-of-a-kind pieces from a Paris fashion show! Unless you travel over there yourself and pay the designer to replicate them, there's nothing you can do to make this up to me!"

I feel my face get red. I do feel bad that I ruined her things. I definitely didn't mean to. I open my mouth, but nothing escapes before she continues.

"Even if you did miraculously track down authentic replicas, I can assure you that you'd still be breaking Lipstick Law Two by what you're wearing right now . . . and pretty much every day. You're a walking clearance rack!"

Erin laughs hysterically. My guilt immediately turns to anger again.

She goes on. "And you broke Lipstick Law Five by not coming clean about lying to me. You were supposed to tell us all of your secrets when you signed the Lipstick Oath!"

"Lying?" I say nervously. Oh no! Did she find out that I'm a bosom sculptor?

"Yeah, you weren't new this year! Why would you lie about that? It's totally creepy! Did you stalk me like a lurking lezzasaurus all last year so you could pounce on me this year? Did you think I wouldn't find out?"

I sink down into the back seat guiltily. "Who told you?"

"Uh . . . did you ever hear of a little thing called a yearbook?"

I'm feeling more uncomfortable and stupid by the second.

"Not to mention," she persists, "you broke Lipstick Law Seven by making decisions that screw our popularity stock . . . like . . ." She clears her throat dramatically. "Hmm . . . I don't know . . . calling the cops on Troy Hoffman!"

"I did not!" I yell.

"Don't lie!" Britney snaps.

Erin looks at me in the rearview mirror and says, "Girls like you are the reason there's an *end* in *friend*. You should probably get out of the car now."

"Get out!" Britney screams.

"Are you serious?" I say bleakly, tears welling in my eyes.

"Serious as suicide." Britney scowls.

Grabbing my stuff, I jump out rapidly, praying that they don't try to run me over. Erin starts her car up. The exhaust surrounds me like I'm going to vanish in a magic act. I wish I *could* vanish.

"Cheers to tears!" Britney cackles out the window as they speed away.

With my face and fingers red from frostbite, I finally bolt through the front door of my house. The heat shocks my system, and I begin to hyperventilate. Luckily, no one's home; the last thing I need at this point is an interrogating Mom intervention. I run up the stairs and slam my bedroom door. I fall onto my bed and cover my head with a frilly pillow. My face is a waterfall. This afternoon, I'm using tissues for my tears rather than my bra. I wait by the phone until school is out in Kansas to call Haley. Now, more than ever, I need to talk to her. I pray she answers her phone. Ever since she met her boyfriend and thinks that I've turned into one of Brit's evil circus clowns, she's been MIA.

A sigh of relief hits me when she picks up her cell. "Hello?"

"Lee!" My voice cracks as I try to hold back tears.

"April, what's wrong?"

I can't hold back the waterworks anymore. I start to cry like a baby.

"Let me guess," she blurts angrily. "Britney Taylor?"

"Yes!" I manage to gurgle out between sniffles and hysteria.

"I won't say I told you so . . ."

"You just did!" I grow more and more upset. "I should've known the minute they started playing the Rank-a-Skank game!"

"That's a pretty big red flag," Haley agrees.

I sob.

I can't take it anymore. I burst into a rambling rant, pacing around my room animatedly. My tongue wrestles with every syllable before spitting out words fiercely into the phone. I tell her everything—every dreadful detail of the last seventy-two hours of my pathetic life.

"Sounds familiar," Haley says sympathetically.

"Familiar?" I say. "If something like this happened to you, *why* didn't you give me the details?"

"It's not like I didn't try to warn you. You've always known what I think of her."

"Yeah, but some specifics would've helped a little!" I say, annoyed beyond belief.

"I told you we had a big falling-out. I figured that was enough to make you want to stay away from her. I've been dead to Britney for years now; why would I want to spend my time rehashing all the horrible details? I wanted to forget it all!"

"But you barely told me anything worth mentioning! What about the Lipstick Laws? If I had known about them, maybe I wouldn't be in this situation right now! How could you leave me in the dark?" I sputter.

"I'm sorry, April. I thought what I told you was enough. I'd never purposefully leave you in the dark."

I roll my eyes. "You told me to stay away from red lipstick . . . How is that helpful to me? By the time the red lipstick was in my face, I didn't have much of a choice!"

There's a short silence before Haley responds. "Honestly, I never talked about the Lipstick Laws because I was embarrassed. I thought you might shun me like they did. And by the time you started becoming friends with them this year, I thought it was too late. You made up your mind. I couldn't change it."

"That's not true, Haley. Anyhow, why would I shun you? You're my best friend."

"Right," Haley says. "You're my best friend now . . . but if you knew that becoming friends with me back then would get you a permanent residency in the penthouse of Loserhood, you probably would've thought twice."

I'm upset and curious at the same time. Haley's been so elusive with details, maybe she'll finally open up about everything now that my life's ruined. But how could she keep the horrors of the Lipstick Laws from me? Yes, I know she vaguely warned me. And yes, I know she told me a little about Britney's wicked ways . . . but I always brushed it off as jealousy. I mean, I never thought anyone could be as bad as Haley was making Brit out to be. But I was wrong. So, maybe this is my fault. Maybe I did know better than to get myself wrapped up with Britney and her clique. I guess my desire for friends and popularity out-weighed Haley's warning. Even if she had filled me in on all the scandalous details of the Lipstick Laws, I'm not sure I would have listened. I'm ready to listen now, though . . . now that it's way too late.

"Well, you might as well spill the Lipstick Law beans now," I say depressingly.

"I guess," she says. "If it'll make you feel better."

"It's a tad late, but it sure couldn't hurt," I say.

"Well, to start, I was best friends with Britney for five years."

"How could you be best friends with the devil's spawn?" I say.

"She wasn't always evil like this. She used to be sweet and funny. She was a really, really good friend. She totally changed when she came back from fat camp."

"Fat camp?" I blurt, totally shocked.

"Yeah, Brit used to be fat," Lee says.

"How fat?" I say, a satisfied smile creeping on my face.

"Not like 'Oh crap, call the fire department, Britney's stuck in the door again' kind of fat . . . but she was chubby enough to be called Donut throughout elementary school," she reveals.

I laugh, picturing Britney as a big jelly-filled donut . . . with strawberry jelly oozing from her mouth onto her designer wardrobe. It's the best daydream I've ever had . . . apart from the one about me and Hottie-Body on a beach in Cabo.

Haley continues, "Her mom fabricated a lie about her dad and blamed Britney for their separation. She told her that her dad was leaving because he was embarrassed about Brit's weight."

"That's awful," I say, temporarily forgetting my disdain for her. "Why would Britney's mom do something like that?"

"I don't know. Maybe it was jealousy over Brit's strong relationship with her father . . . or maybe embarrassment over her failed marriage? Who knows. I think he left her for a friend or something like that. She probably wanted to project the blame onto her daughter so she wouldn't have to deal with reality." Haley sighs heavily. "If you haven't noticed, Brit's mom is just as conniving and image-obsessed as her daughter's become."

Don't get me wrong; I still can't stand Britney, but this revelation gives me an understanding of where she's learned her interpersonal skills. It doesn't change the fact that she's a living nightmare, but it's definitely sad, to say the least. Putting all that's happened aside, I feel sorry for the young Donut-nicknamed Britney in a detached sort of way.

"So, Britney believed her mother? How could she believe that? Her dad loves her, right?" I ask.

"Of course he loves her. He spoils her rotten!"

"I know," I agree, thinking of her brand-new car, stacked designer wardrobe, and expensive handbag collection.

"Her mom was persistent and convincing. She had been trying to get Brit to lose weight for years. She was the one embarrassed by her, not her father. I guess the prospect of the divorce was the perfect opportunity to make Brit's weight disappear. She knew how much Britney adored her father and that she'd do anything in her means to persuade him to stay. And she did. Britney went to fat camp for the whole summer before sixth grade. She came back a new person—inside and out."

"Wow," I say. "The evolution of a monster . . . I never woulda thought it all started at fat camp."

Haley laughs. "Me either."

"So, what happened next?"

"Well, Britney was absolutely destroyed when she got back from camp to find that her parents' divorce had been finalized. She created the Lipstick Laws soon after."

"Were you there? Did you help her create them?" I question curiously.

"No, I didn't help her create the Lipstick Laws! Are you kidding? I thought they were ridiculous. But I agreed to follow them, 'cause she was my best friend . . . and they seemed important to her. Honestly, I thought it was just a weird phase she was going through. Little did I know, it wasn't a phase . . . and the Lipstick Laws would eventually come between us."

"After five years she let those absurd laws ruin your friendship?"

"Yeah, but remember, I was friends with the old Britney for all those years . . . not the new one," Haley says. "You wanna know the most ironic part of the story?"

"What?" I ask, sitting on the edge of my bed in anticipation.

"She kicked me out in eighth grade for breaking Lipstick Law Three."

I gasp. "The weight law?"

"Yes! I was a month shy of my first period . . . so, understandably, I was a bloated mess. But Brit didn't care how or why I gained weight. She said, 'Weight gain is a choice, and I can't be friends with someone who makes bad choices.'"

"What a bitchawitch!" I say. "You were friends with her while she was a donut!"

"I know. You'd think she'd stick by me 'cause I stuck by her . . . but instead, she said the only friend I needed was Jenny Craig. I was devastated!"

"This makes me loathe her even more," I seethe.

Haley is the sweetest person I've ever met. How could any- one do something like that to her? I was only friends with Brit for a few months. But Haley was friends with her for five years. Getting dumped by a long-term best friend had to hurt like a mother-trucker. I feel like crying—not for me, but for poor Haley!

"Don't loathe her, April," Haley says. "Get even."

"Uh . . . how?"

"You need to do what I didn't. You can't let her win. I totally gave her the upper hand by letting her get to me. My mom had my counselor switch my lunch period and classes around so I could avoid her . . . and I became the biggest hermit in the whole northern hemisphere. I even contemplated switching schools until my dad found out about his job transfer. At that point, I knew I only had to get through freshman year, and then I'd be out like a scout."

"That's why you were so happy to meet me last year," I say, putting the pieces of the puzzle together in my head.

"Yeah," she says. "I needed a friend as much as you did. Now you'll understand why I didn't want to jinx our friendship by giving you all the humiliating Lipstick Law details. I couldn't risk you seeing me the way they did."

"I'd never think badly of you, Lee," I say with a hurt heart. Everything starts making sense to me. I always wondered why such a sweet, pretty girl didn't have any other close friends. It's because she was a victim of the girls and their stupid Lipstick Laws when I met her. I can't help but wonder if that's my future, too. My stomach churns with distress.

"Well, what do you suggest I do now? I can't live out the rest of my high school career as a Lipstick Law reject!"

"You need to fight back!" Haley insists. "She's done this to too many girls to get away with it again."

"There are others like us?"

"Of course, there are plenty of Lipstick Law casualties! Sure, the girls I know of were run out of the school . . . like Andrea Birman, Stacy Rosco, and Emma Jenkins."

"Tube socks Emma?" I blurt, looking down at my padded chest.

"Yes, tube socks Emma. I heard they made her life miserable before she left. I'm sure there are probably a handful of girls that are still there, though . . . hating life and their misfit curse." She pauses before exclaiming, "You should all get together and create an underground society! You can call yourselves the Lipstick Lawbreakers!"

The wheels in my head begin to turn at this genius idea.

chapter nine

The next day, I find myself sitting across from Darci Madison's boobage again. It's sort of hard to swallow my pride and ride the bus when I'd gotten used to Erin driving me to school. I notice that Darci's looking more conservative lately. I feel bad for ranking her a five on the skank scale.

Haley's voice pops in my mind: "There are plenty of other Lipstick Law casualties."

I wonder if Darci is one of them. I'm staring at her, trying to picture if Britney would have been friends with her at some point. She catches me staring, so I look away for a moment. After a minute or two, I lean into the aisle, deciding that I have to ask her.

"Hey, Darci, are you a Lipstick Lawbreaker?"

She stares back at me blankly. "A what?"

"A Lipstick Lawbreaker," I repeat. "You know, the 'Lipstick Oath,'" I say, using finger quotes.

"Uh . . . I don't think so . . . No. Definitely not!" she responds, looking unusually shocked.

I have an overwhelming suspicion that she thinks I'm asking her if she's a lesbian. I wonder if she thinks I'm trying to pick her up.

I lean back over and say, "I'm not a lesbian."

"Ummm . . . okay. That's fine," she says uncomfortably.

I analyze her stunned expression and quickly add, "Not that there's anything wrong with that. You know . . . being a lesbian and all. Not that I am one or anything."

"Right," she says, inching closer to the window, using her backpack as a blockade between us.

The rest of the ride is really awkward.

As I get close to my locker, I see that a small crowd has formed around it. Some are pointing, some are whispering to each other . . . but most are laughing. I brush them away and see the most stomach-sickening sight: a bunch of tampons taped to my locker, slathered with thick, bright red waxy goop. The words SKUNK SKANK are scribbled with the same gloppy stuff. It doesn't take me long to realize the goop is the Lipstick Oath lipstick. Tears fill my eyes. My face bubbles with humiliation heat, surely turning bright red like the lipstick. I'm embarrassed beyond belief.

A minute after the hall has emptied for first period, I hear the clanking of dress shoes behind me.

"See. Right there."

"Thank you, Angie."

Out of the corner of my eye I see a small freshman scurry off. She looks back a few times before turning the corner.

"April?" A woman's voice tries to get my attention.

It doesn't work. My tampered locker is like a magnet. I can't bear to turn around.

"April?" She taps my shoulder.

There's a delay, but eventually I respond quietly without breaking my gaze. "Yeah?"

I'm horrified when I see that the chair in the principal's office is just a shade darker than the lipstick on my locker. Those biatches have ruined the color red for me.

"April, do you know who did this?"

Of course I know! I know exactly who did this! I even know the exact lipstick she used! However, I shake my head no, knowing that tattling is a cardinal sin in high school—almost worse than being a complete loser.

"Please, honey, look at me," Mrs. Wagner says compassionately. Tears fall from my eyes as I look up at her. "I know this is hard, but if you know who did this, you have to tell me. I will not tolerate this behavior in my school. The person responsible for this needs to be punished!"

My chin trembles; I open my mouth to speak, but nothing comes out. She hands me a tissue and continues, "Whoever it is doesn't need to know that you told me."

I know she knows that I know. Looking down, I shake my head again, mumbling, "I don't know, Mrs. Wagner."

I go through the rest of the day like a complete zombie. I don't answer teachers in class, I don't go to lunch, I don't try to talk to Jessica in Spanish class, and I don't even do my normal Tuesday walk-by to spy on Matt in his gym class. It's like I'm not even here at all—exactly how I want it to be.

As depressingly aloof as I've been all day, I'm able to focus on the video about World War II in ninth-period history. The soldier carrying a grenade on the screen suddenly morphs into Britney Taylor hauling a massive tampon. I rub my eyes repeatedly and take another look. It's back to the black-and-white war clip. Great, now I'm seeing things.

Mr. Stuart strolls by my desk, casually dropping me a note: SEE ME AFTER CLASS FOR DETENTION. I'm not surprised; I skipped his class yesterday. What I *am* surprised about is that he hasn't humiliated me in front of the class. Even Mr. Gladiator Man has more tact than Britney.

"So?" Mr. Stuart says after all the other students have left for the day. "I think you have some explaining to do."

I remain tightlipped at my desk, sliding my shoe in circles on the floor below.

"April, I know you were in school yesterday. You're in my homeroom, remember?" He gets up from behind his desk and walks over to me. His massive frame surrounds me in a shadow of doom. "Where were you ninth period yesterday?"

Feeling word-vomit creeping up my throat, I blurt, "I was with people who I thought were friends, getting my life ruined!"

My hand slaps over my mouth immediately. *Oops! Did I just say that?*

Mr. Stuart steps back, clearly not expecting what he heard. "Well, regardless of why . . . you need to put your time in here at detention."

He walks back to his desk.

Shocking. I really expected him to have a major freak-out fest over this. I mean, everyone knows he's crazier than a shaved mule in a toboggan race. This is definitely not the response I predicted. Feeling relieved but somewhat skeptical, I cover my head on my desk in mourning. Mourning for my life lost to the Lipstick Laws.

Halfway through my forty-five-minute prison sentence, I haven't lifted my head once, until I'm startled by Mr. Stuart's deep voice.

"You know, I wasn't always this big, tough football coach," he says nonchalantly while grading a paper at his desk.

I look around, wondering if someone else slipped in the room while I was grieving.

He looks up from his paper at me. "You hear me?"

"Yes?" I say, not knowing where he's going with this.

"I hated high school," he says. "Nope, ya couldn't pay me to go back . . ." He grins. "As a student, that is."

"What do you mean?"

"I didn't play football in high school. I was the ball. Kicked around like you wouldn't believe." He grimaces at the thought.

"Really?" I say in disbelief.

"Really! I know it's hard to believe now . . . with these guns and all." He points to his huge biceps and laughs.

I laugh too. This is the most human I've ever seen Mr. Stuart. Maybe he's not the roid-raging monster that I thought he was.

"Remember, April, high school doesn't last forever. It'll be over before you know it. Let what you go through today motivate you to become a stronger person tomorrow. That's what I did, and look at me. The guys that kicked me around then would run from me now." He grins proudly and returns to grading the paper.

"Thanks," I mumble. I'm not sure if he hears me, though. I stare at him, trying to imagine him as a bullied kid. It's completely impossible to even picture it. Something that he said rings true to me. Britney Taylor and her stupid Lipstick Laws don't define me. Ten years from now, I'm not going to have a lipstick-smudged tampon taped to my forehead. Or at least I hope not . . .

Suddenly motivated to do what I had talked about with Haley yesterday, I decide that it's time to fight back. I'm a Lipstick Lawbreaker, and I'm going to dethrone Britney and her Lipstick Laws if it's the last thing I do!

With my remaining detention time, I try to devise a plan. How can I connect with other Lipstick Lawbreakers? I can't very well go around asking all the girls in school if they broke the Lipstick Laws. I mean, Darci Madison already thinks I'm crazy for my shenanigans on the bus today. Obviously, I'll have to get them to come to me somehow . . . but how do I manage that without Britney finding out? Then, out of nowhere, the answer comes to me.

"The school newspaper!" I blurt out excitedly.

Mr. Stuart jumps. "You okay, April?"

Oops . . . didn't mean to say that out loud. "Sorry, just talking to myself."

Puzzled, he returns to his work.

Brilliant idea! Britney and the girls wouldn't be caught dead reading the school newspaper. I'll put an ad in the section on the back page where people advertise for clubs. I'll ask them to run the ad for a couple of weeks, giving enough time for other Lipstick Lawbreakers to see it. But where should the first meeting take place? I can't very well advertise my address . . . that wouldn't be too smart. I rack my brain for ideas. For obvious reasons, it can't be anywhere in the school. And the Lawlords live at the mall, so that's out. It has to be somewhere that they would never go. I've got it—I elect not to announce my idea to Mr. Stuart this time—the Penford Public Library!

I use the last ten minutes of detention to write up a clever ad. Something that only other Lipstick Lawbreakers will understand:

Attention Lipstick Lawbreakers:

Was the Oath not all you thought it would be?
Did you wear the wrong clothes? Did you hide too many secrets?
Or maybe your decisions were too unique
to appeal to the Lawlords?
Are you sick of being cast as a social misfit
and ready to take a stand?
Whatever your Lipstick Lawbreaking story may be,
come meet others just like you.
We can make a difference together!
Meeting Date: December 12th
Meeting Time: 7pm
Meeting Place: Penford Public Library (the back table)
Dress Code: Wear anything but the color red!

chapter ten

After sitting alone at the Penford Public Library for a while, I begin to wonder if this was a bad idea. It's three minutes before seven, and I've only seen a few people back here: a frustrated young mother trying to catch her sugar-high child, a librarian putting away reference books, and a cute elderly lady looking for bird watching books.

It's 6:59—still nobody. Maybe they'll be right on time.

Nope, 7:02—still alone. I guess they could be running a few minutes late. The weather *is* bad today.

Tapping my finger impatiently, I start to feel really foolish for thinking this would work. I try to distract myself with a book; however, my watch keeps calling my name. It's 7:10 now. I should probably admit defeat. Feeling embarrassed, I've started gathering my stuff to leave when a soft voice interrupts me . . .

"Ummm . . . hi. Is this supposed to be a meeting?"

I look up to see Melanie Elmer standing in front of me. I suddenly remember she was best friends with Britney last year. They were practically attached at the hip. She has to be in the right place. I'm giddy with excitement!

"Yes!" I say. "You mean, from the ad in the school paper, right?"

She nods. Relief releases the tension in her cheeks. She smiles and says, "I'm a Lipstick Lawbreaker."

A few seconds later, two other girls show up together. Melanie and I greet them with welcoming smiles.

"Is this the Lipstick Lawbreaker meeting?" they inquire.

"Yes," I say. "Thanks for coming!"

"I'm Ashley, and this is Rachel." Rachel waves as they sit down.

Melanie and I introduce ourselves. I can already tell that I'm going to like all three of these girls. They're certainly not the suffering misfits that Britney has referred to.

"I guess we should wait a little longer before we start. Maybe more people are coming," I say.

"Yeah, it's half a blizzard out there. I would've been on time, but I had to scrape ice off my car," Melanie says, taking off her scarf and gloves.

"I think someone else is coming." I point to a tall figure emerging from the rows of books. The closer she comes, the more peculiar she looks.

"Oh my!" Rachel exclaims.

"Interesting outfit," Ashley mumbles.

Melanie's mouth hangs open. She whispers, "Is that a guy in women's clothing?"

"I think it is," I mutter, admiring the superb job he's done stuffing his bra.

"Is this the Lipstick Lawbreaker meeting?" his deep voice croaks. When he brushes the long blond wig from his face, he suddenly realizes that four girls . . . four real girls . . . are sitting in front of him.

"Hey! Wait a second. What's going on?" he asks.

"You tell us!" I laugh.

Clearly disappointed, he says, "This isn't a cross-dressing club, is it?"

"No!" we reply in sync.

Looking uneasy, he explains, "You know, I just thought when I read the ad . . . I mean, it was sorta misleading. Lipstick Lawbreakers . . . wrong clothes . . . unique decisions . . . hiding secrets . . . social misfit . . . yadda-yadda . . . you get the idea. Um, so . . . I guess I was wrong."

Melanie recognizes him. "Mark? I never knew . . ."

"Oh! Hey, Mel! Ummmm . . . Let's, ah . . . let's just pretend this never happened. I'm gonna get going," he murmurs, adjusting his periwinkle blouse as he stumbles away in high heels.

Stunned, we all stare at each other in disbelief.

Melanie breaks the silence. "It's pretty sad that Mark Rhinehart puts on makeup better than I do. That guy deserves some serious props."

We burst into laughter. Five minutes later, we begin to compose ourselves. Our faces are purple, and our stomachs are sore from laughing.

"Do you think anyone else is coming?" I giggle.

"I don't think my sides can handle any more surprise guests," Rachel says, holding her stomach.

"So, I guess we can get things started now," I say, thankful for the unpredictable opening. After all, laughter is always the best icebreaker.

"Obviously we all have a couple things in common," I say, looking around at the girls. "We all signed the Lipstick Oath at some point. And at some point after that, we all broke a Lipstick Law and got kicked out of the group by the head Lipstick Lawlord . . . Britney Taylor. Am I right?"

I glance around at three nodding heads.

"Yes," they say.

"But I'm sure our Lipstick Lawbreaking stories aren't all the same," I add. "And I feel like the best place to start is to hear everyone's story. After that, we can figure out what we want to do from there. If nothing else, this is a great way to come together and vent."

Melanie smiles. "I'm dying to hear everyone's story! I've felt like I'm going through this all on my own. It's nice to be around people who can relate."

"I totally agree," I say. "So, who wants to start?"

"I'll start," Rachel says swiftly, taking a deep breath before beginning her story. "I became close friends with Britney Taylor in eighth grade. She had just gotten in a big fight with her science partner and asked our teacher to switch partners. Lucky me, right?"

I secretly wonder if the science partner Rachel's referring to was Haley. I bet it was.

Rachel continues. "I was friends with Britney for a month before she asked me to sign the Lipstick Oath. Things were okay at first until my mom lost her job. We were kind of struggling for a while and I wanted to help out. Obviously, no one would hire me at thirteen, so I decided to sell some of my stuff on eBay. Britney was horror-struck when she found out that I sold a lot of my nicest clothes. She said I was breaking Lipstick Laws One and Two, and immediately kicked me out."

"That's terrible!" Melanie says.

"I know . . . it was! And I'm sure you guys can relate; she made my life hell after that. One day, she came up to me in lunch . . . and I was hopeful she wanted to be friends again. Instead, she handed me a five-dollar gift certificate to the Dollar

Closet and told me to go buy a new wardrobe. Then she got half the school to call me DC."

"What does that mean?" I ask.

"It stands for Dollar Closet." She shudders.

Melanie and I gasp.

"That's so mean!" I say.

Rachel points to Ashley. "I wouldn't have survived it all without her."

"So, what's your story?" Melanie and I switch our attention to Ashley.

"Well, I've been friends with Rachel forever, and she convinced me to sign the Lipstick Oath." She looks at Rachel, scrunching her nose. "Shortly after I took the Oath, the group turned on Rachel. And Britney demanded that I drop her, too. When I wouldn't stop talking to her, Brit flipped out, saying I was breaking Lipstick Law Four. She kicked me out at the end of eighth grade—"

Rachel interjects, "After Britney kicked me out, she considered me a member of the geek kingdom and didn't want anyone talking to me . . . even my best friend."

"That seems to be the norm," Melanie says.

"Well, I wasn't about to drop Rachel." Ashley shakes her head incredulously. "Why would I choose Britney Taylor over my best friend since kindergarten? I only signed the Lipstick Oath for Rachel to begin with."

Rachel looks at Ashley and smiles. It's nice to see that friendships can survive the Lipstick Laws. It seems like it may have even made them closer.

"So, how about you?" Ashley points to Melanie.

"Oh gosh, where do I start?" Melanie sighs heavily. "I met Brit at a pool party the summer before freshman year. It was actually Brianna's party."

"Lipstick Law Brianna? Bri Thompson?" I say.

"Yeah, Lipstick Law Brianna. Believe it or not, Bri and I had been friends for a while before she got infatuated with Britney. She was pretty cool back then."

"I just can't picture her not infatuated with Brit," I say.

Melanie agrees. "I know what you mean! After they met, Britney was all Brianna would talk about. She was obsessed with fitting in with her. She dressed like her, tried to talk like her, and even acted like her—it was kind of pathetic. Obviously, after all the talk, I was really curious to meet Britney. I always knew who she was, but I never really talked to her . . . until Brianna's party. After that, Brit called me every day to hang out. By the time school started in September, we were super close . . . and Brianna was super jealous! She was so mad when she found out that I signed the Lipstick Oath and she wasn't asked to sign it."

"I can imagine!" I say.

"Yeah, Brianna became more and more frustrated with every passing month . . . and no Lipstick Law invite. I guess she got so fed up and jealous that she decided to stab me in the back."

"What'd she do?" we ask, wide-eyed.

"She made up this elaborate story about me trying to get with Britney's ex-boyfriend Brad Miller." Melanie shakes her head. "It was a total lie, but you know how crazy Britney is about friends flirting with her exes."

"You know her father left her mom for her mom's best friend, right?" Rachel reveals.

"I heard something like that," I say. "But Erin told me he took off with some random woman."

Melanie shakes her head. "No, Rachel's right. It's a big family secret. That's why Brit's so particular about Lipstick Law Six. Her mother has stamped it into her head not to trust her friends . . . even though she won't fully admit that he left her for one. Now Britney doesn't even trust when her friends make eye contact with someone she likes."

"Wow," I mutter, realizing that Lipstick Law Six has more significance than I had originally thought. Although I can't stand Britney, that's a pretty crappy thing for her father to do. "I know her dad supposedly really loves her, but that's not a very good way to show it."

"I know . . . but really, could you blame him for wanting to escape from Britney's mom? She's a nightmare." Ashley laughs.

"Yeah, but Britney got a bum deal in it all," I say, empathizing with BFC (Before Fat Camp) Britney again.

"That's probably why she's so messed up. Now that he has a new family with his new wife, the only real love Britney feels from her father is through his expensive gifts," Melanie explains with a frown.

"Maybe that's why she's so materialistic. Her value is in things, not herself," I say, trying to make sense of her wicked ways.

The girls nod at this revelation.

"Taking her background into account," Melanie continues, "you can imagine how quickly Brit kicked me out once she thought I was going behind her back with Brad. Even though I would never do anything like that."

"Did she leave you alone afterward?" Ashley asks.

"Does Britney ever leave anyone alone?" Melanie rolls her eyes. "Once you're on her radar, you're done for. Britney made my life a nightmare. And once Brianna was asked to sign the Oath, she harassed me even more than Brit did. During the last week of school last year they sent a letter to my parents addressed like it came from Mrs. Wagner. It said that I was being expelled from school for being a Skunk Skank. I was mortified!"

"The dreaded Rank-a-Skank scale," I say. "What did your parents do?"

"They were so mad! They took it to the principal's office, and Mrs. Wagner was super furious too! Of course, she wanted to punish whoever did it. I acted like I didn't know who sent it, though. I was too embarrassed and sort of scared about what Britney or Brianna might do if I told, you know?"

"Trust me, I know," I agree, thinking this story hits too close to home.

"Okay, April, you're the only one left. Time to reveal all the skeletons in your closet. You can't break Lipstick Law Five! We need to know all of your secrets!" Melanie jokes.

"Ha! That's one of the laws I broke," I say. "And get this, now there's going to be a Lipstick Law Eight because of me."

The girls lean in to me curiously. "What is it?"

"Never ditch a friend at a party, leaving her hiding from the cops in a dirty laundry basket," I say with a smirk.

Everyone cracks up.

"Oh! I gotta hear the reasoning behind this one!" Melanie claps her hands.

I tell them everything—the party, the cops, Brandon "Chin Hair" Smith, the tourniquet shoes, the herpes argument . . .

even the tampon bit. It's everything that has already been whispered about in the hallways of Penford High School . . . but from my side of the story, down to the tiniest, most brutal details.

They look at me, stunned.

"Your Lipstick Lawbreaker story takes the cake," Ashley says with admiration.

I nod. "What can I say . . . 'Go big or go home,' right?"

They laugh.

"Now that we've found each other, we should seriously make a pact to stick together. Maybe we can fight back and beat Britney at her own game," Melanie suggests with a sly grin.

"I'm on the same page," I say. "Britney deserves a taste of her own medicine."

We all agree to our new Lipstick Lawbreaker pact. After another hour of talking and laughing about crazy Lipstick Law stories, I leave the library beaming with happiness. I just made three new friends. Three new nice friends. Maybe breaking the Lipstick Laws wasn't such a bad thing.

chapter eleven

On the last day of school before Christmas break, I'm totally shocked when Jessica follows me out of Spanish class and starts talking.

"Hey, April," she says. "I noticed you're sitting with Melanie Elmer at lunch now."

I'm caught off-guard. Why has Jessica been watching me?

"Yes?" I say cautiously.

"Will you tell her I said hi?"

Annoyed, I snap, "Are you joking, Jessica?"

"No," she says sincerely. "Mel's nice . . . I always liked her."

"Aren't you breaking a bunch of Lipstick Laws by talking about this with me?"

"Well"—she pauses—"kinda. Brit would have a fit if she knew, but she doesn't have to know."

I immediately grow suspicious.

She continues, "You know, I don't agree with everything Britney does."

"Like?" I inquire.

She looks down. "Well, like . . . take you, for instance. The whole tampon thing . . . that was a bit much."

"You think?" I huff sarcastically.

"I didn't have anything to do with that," she says adamantly, shaking her head. "And another thing, I know you didn't call the cops on Troy Hoffman."

Feeling vindicated, I say, "How'd you figure that out?"

"I talked to Brandon about it. Didn't you wonder why that rumor was squashed? I told people it wasn't you."

"You did?" I say skeptically, studying her dark eyes for signs of lying.

"Of course I did. Well, I'll let you get to class," she says casually before walking away.

—————

"Shut up!" Melanie blurts, practically choking on her gum. "You have to be kidding!"

"No, I'm not," I say. "And she told me to tell you hi."

"That's so random, I don't even know how to react to it."

"That's what I thought," I agree.

"I mean, out of all of them she was always the nicest. But I still wouldn't trust her."

"No, I definitely don't," I say, buckling my seat belt. "She hasn't talked to me for weeks. I don't know what made her talk to me today. It's really weird!"

Mel looks in the rearview before backing up. "Maybe Bratney's driving her crazy."

"That's the only driving she's good at," I say.

As Mel pulls out of the school parking lot, I grind my teeth, thinking of all the things Britney has done to me over the past month. The last incident was the straw that broke the camel's back. It took me a year to get those jeans worn in perfectly. They were like my skin, they were so comfortable.

Melanie glances over at me.

"You're still thinking about the jeans, aren't you?" she says.

"Yes!" I churn with irritation.

I knew that Britney was up to something when she excused herself for a long bathroom break during gym class earlier this week. Call it Lipstick Lawbreaker intuition, but I just knew she was up to no good. I still don't know how she broke in to my new locker, but that doesn't matter at this point. It's what she did once she broke in that I'm still fuming about.

"Did you try patching it?"

"No, Mel. They're ruined. You saw them! The hole is way too big . . . and where am I going to find a crotch patch?"

Mel tries to lighten my mood. "That's true. There aren't nearly enough crotch patch stores nowadays."

I manage to laugh, though I'm still flaring inside.

Mel parks at the drugstore. Snowflakes swarm us. We slip on the snow slush as we make our way through the parking lot. Grabbing on to each other for warmth, we walk into the store and dash for the makeup aisle. Once we find what we stopped for, Mel and I head to the checkout. She picks out a juicy gossip magazine at the front counter. Her hazel eyes shimmer with mischief as she flips through it.

"Hollywood marriages never work out." She shakes her head grimly.

I look at her and laugh. Melanie is as addicted to gossip columns as I am to bosom sculpting. She's even said that she hopes to be a Hollywood marriage therapist someday. Talk about mixing work with pleasure. It's nice to know that I have a friend as obsessively neurotic as myself.

"What?" she says, gaping at me. "I just can't resist. It's my guilty pleasure, this and reality TV."

She promptly adds it to the register.

Fifteen minutes later, Mel, Ashley, Rachel, and I are congregated on my bed. After being kicked out of the public library twice for laughing too hard and "disturbing library patrons," we moved our Lipstick Lawbreaker meetings to my house.

"So," Ashley says, "where is it?"

"Here!" I pull out our lipstick purchase from the plastic bag.

Ashley leans in to get a better look. "Oh—wow! It's really dark!"

"Midnight black," Melanie announces. "Can't get much darker than that."

"Perfect shade for you, Apes. Mr. Hottie-Body Brentwood won't be able to resist asking you to the spring formal if you've got this on," Rachel teases, inspecting the goth color.

His name sends my mind somewhere else. Somewhere romantic. Somewhere tropical. A place where he can show off his delicious body on a beach—in a swimsuit or, preferably, his birthday suit. I can't even imagine not seeing him over Christmas break. After the whole Brandon Smith hoo-ha, it took me a few weeks to get Matt to talk to me. Unfortunately for me, as soon as we were on good terms again, he and his family left for a blistery Colorado vacation. If only I could have hidden in his suitcase . . . just to sneak a glance at him snowboarding. Yummy von yumster . . .

Melanie snaps her fingers in my face. "That name puts you in a trance every time. Snap outta it!"

I shrug. "Sorry, can't help it. He's a love god."

"Yeah, yeah . . . we know." Rachel tucks her shoulder-length hair behind her ears. "So, do you have the Oath?"

"Of course!" I say, skipping to my dresser.

The girls watch intently as I snatch the piece of paper and dangle it with a smile.

"Britney isn't gonna know what hit 'er," I say, adding a dramatically evil laugh. "Mmwwahh-ha-ha-ha."

I wiggle between them and jump up on my bed. My feet sink slightly into the mattress. Standing as tall as I can, I clear my throat and read:

> "Lipstick Lawbreaker Law:
> Destroy Britney Taylor!"

We put our right hands up simultaneously and repeat our new Lipstick Lawbreaker Oath:

"We, the Lipstick Lawbreakers, pledge our commitment to destroy Britney Taylor. We promise to follow our Lipstick Lawbreaker Law, knowing that her misery is dependent on our ability to fulfill it."

I bounce down to sit in the middle of the girls. I cross my legs and say, "Pass the lipstick, please."

One by one, we each smear the black lipstick on our lips and kiss our new Lipstick Lawbreaker Oath under its one incredibly important law.

"I can't believe we're doing this!" Melanie says.

"It's about time," I respond.

Later that night, as I'm washing off the last bit of black lipstick, my brother approaches me, leaning his tall, lanky body on the wall outside the bathroom door.

I shoot him a don't-mess-with-me look from the bathroom mirror.

He stares back at me seriously.

"What, Aaden?" I accidentally spit soap bubbles onto my shirt.

"We haven't talked about this yet, but I know what she did to you." He walks closer to me. "What Britney did to you."

My heart stops. I rinse and wipe my face off. "How do you know?"

"Um . . . it's pretty common knowledge," he responds.

"Perfect!" I say bluntly, passing him to escape to my bedroom.

"Wait, Apers." He grabs my shoulder. I haven't heard him call me that since we were little. I don't turn around, but I'm listening. "I just want to let you know that after what she did to you, I don't think she's hot anymore. She's actually really ugly . . . really, really ugly!"

I'm smiling inside. Aaden has always thought Britney's one of the hottest girls in high school. He was more than baffled when his kid sister started hanging out with her. I caught him smelling her jacket in the hallway one time when she came to our house. It was totally creepy in a Delvin McGerk stalkerific way. So, naturally, I'm shocked by his anti-Britney sentiments.

"She sucks," he adds unwaveringly.

"Thanks, Aaden," I say, spinning around to give him a big hug . . . which turns out to be a bit mechanical and awkward.

He blushes. "Anyway, Melanie Elmer is hands down hotter than Britney Taylor."

"You got that right!" I say.

Mel and Brit look like they could be sisters. Like Cinderella and her evil stepsister. Mel being Cinderella, of course. And in this case, I'm hoping the evil stepsister gets what's coming to her.

chapter twelve

"Good afternoon, Bean!" My father greets me from his mahogany desk as I come down the garland-decorated stairway. That's been his nickname for me since I was born. Supposedly I was a small, round, overly gassy baby.

"Morning, Dad," I respond, wiping the sleep from my eyes.

"It's not morning anymore, my darlin'." He laughs. "Ah, to be a teenager again . . . when noon is morning and midnight is going to bed early."

I look at the clock in his study and see that it's twelve-thirty in the afternoon already. Melanie and I were on the phone until three a.m. last night. We came up with a fantastic plan to speed up the destruction of Britney Taylor. I can't wait to share it with Haley.

"Where's Mom?"

My dad points to the kitchen. "Attempting to make cookies."

Oh, boy—this could be a disaster. I follow the scent of burnt cookies into the kitchen and immediately see an explosion of baking supplies all over the counters, and a bunch of half-charred cookies cooling on the island. My mom definitely tries, but she's no domestic goddess.

"Do you need help baking, Mom?" I say, assessing the kitchen nightmare.

She dismisses my offer with a quick wave of her oven mitt. "No, thanks. I just have one more batch to bake."

Knowing raw sugar-cookie dough always tastes better than the overcooked end product, I snag a bite and stop to admire the holiday card photos plastered like wallpaper on our fridge. I point to the middle picture. "Who's this hottie?"

My mom looks surprised. "April, that's Delvin McGerk. Don't you recognize him?"

I gag on the dough and zone in closer to the picture. "Can't be!"

"Sure is; Patty McGerk sent that to me earlier this week. Handsome, isn't he?"

Delvin McGerk, handsome? That's the last word I'd use to describe him. A good-looking imposter must have fooled the camera. There's definitely some sort of trickery going on. That's the only explanation.

"He must've got contacts," I say.

My mom admires the flattering picture over my shoulder. "Yes, he got his braces off, too."

"And a full face overhaul," I mutter under my breath.

"Be nice, April! Delvin's a sweet boy."

"Right." I roll my eyes and grab a granola bar before heading back upstairs.

I'm clutching the Lipstick Lawbreaker Oath tightly as I dial Haley's number. She's going to be so proud.

"April!"

"Your caller ID is fixed," I reply.

"Yep, thank goodness! Now I can screen Jordan's calls," she says.

The last time I talked to her, I was surprised to hear that she broke things off with her boyfriend. Supposedly, he went a little psycho over a breakfast Eggo a few days ago. Long story . . . but the moral of it is that you know it's over when maple syrup makes your boyfriend crazy.

"We signed the Oath!" I say.

"You did? I'm so excited! Did you guys think up any ideas yet?"

I lie on my bed, twisting the drawstring from my hoodie around my fingers. "Mel and I thought of an awesome idea last night."

"Tell me!"

"Well . . . what does Britney want more than anything?" I hint.

"Ummm . . . I dunno . . . a herd of brainless followers?" Haley says.

"Well . . . yeah. But what else?"

"Hmmm . . . every guy in the universe to worship her?"

"That's true too," I say, figuring this guessing game could go on all day if I don't just come out and tell her. "But she's in love with Troy Hoffman, remember?"

"You're right!"

"And Jamie, Troy's girlfriend, hates her," I add.

"Right," she agrees.

"And she's dating Kyle Smith right now . . ."

"Ummm . . . okay," Haley says.

I don't think she gets where I'm going with this.

"Don't you see, Lee? We're gonna set her up to think Troy's into her! If we're successful, we'll destroy her relationship with Kyle, prompt a Jamie/Britney brawl, and demote her popularity rank in the school!"

"Brilliant!" she says. "Don't say *if*. You will be successful! Think good thoughts!" She pauses for a second. "But how are you gonna make her believe Troy likes her without her suspecting you guys?"

"We already figured that all out," I explain. "Melanie knows of an empty locker down the hall from Troy's locker. It's going to become their secret love note mailbox. We'll slip the first note from fake Troy into Britney's actual locker. It'll tell her to leave her reply letters in the empty locker. She'll never know that we're behind it all."

"But, won't she wonder why Troy doesn't just use his own locker to get her love letters?"

"We have that covered, too," I boast. "He doesn't want Jamie to find out, of course. Jamie's constantly hanging out at his locker. That's why this secret letter affair has to take place somewhere else."

"Perfect!" Haley says. "So, how are you going to end everything?"

"This is the best part." I prepare her for the genius. "We plan on making copies of all of Brit's letters. You know she's going to slam Jamie in them, and she'll probably admit that her feelings for Kyle aren't anything compared to her feelings for Troy. Once we have enough criminal evidence, we'll slip her letters to

Jamie and Kyle—which should make for the showdown of the century!"

"Oh my gosh, April! That's amazing! I hope it works!"

"I'm confident it'll work, Lee. Very confident!"

Every time I pass through the kitchen, I find myself staring in disbelief at Delvin's picture. Christmas morning is no exception. He didn't look like that in science class, did he? No way, he couldn't have. Then again, I try not to look at him ever, so I probably wouldn't have noticed even if he did have a miraculous makeover. I shrug and walk into the family room to join the others to exchange gifts.

I sit between my mother, who's bursting with holiday cheer, and Aaden, who'd much rather be sleeping.

I assess the pile of presents as my dad rustles around the tree. He turns around holding two matching, brightly wrapped boxes. My brother and I immediately perk up when my dad hands one to each of us. There's only one present Aaden and I are both hoping for. We look at each other optimistically and tear the wrapping paper to bits.

"Yes—I knew it! It's about time!" Aaden shrieks, doing a happy dance.

"A cell phone!" I dash to my dad and give him a bear hug. "Thank you!"

"Now just remember, this is a trial," my dad warns. "If you two can't control your dialing and texting, you'll be saying goodbye to your cells again."

As soon as the phone is out of the box and in my hands, I text Haley, Mel, Ashley, and Rachel:

> Merry Xmas! OMG—got
> a new cell! TG! TTYL!

Later that night, while sugar plums dance in my head, I have the most amazing dream. Mr. Hottie-Body Brentwood is holding mistletoe over my head. I lustfully admire his bulging bicep and demand that he put his strong arms tightly around me. We fall into a passionate kiss. All the while, in the background, Britney Taylor is roasting like chestnuts on an open fire.

chapter thirteen

Winter break goes by quickly, like all school breaks do. This time, though, I don't mind because I can't wait to enforce our Lipstick Lawbreaker plan. And more important, I can't wait to see Mr. Hottie-Body Brentwood!

"How was your break?" Matt asks as he walks me to my gym class.

"Pretty good," I say. "The real question is, how was your break? Mr. Colorado snowboarder . . ." I nudge him flirtatiously while we weave through the crowded hallway.

"The slopes were amazing. I didn't want to leave."

"You mean you didn't even want to come home to see little ol' me?" I bat my eyelashes playfully.

"Hmm . . ." He puts both hands up like a balance scale. "April, slopes, April, slopes, April . . . Okay, you win!"

"Phew!" I pretend to wipe sweat from my brow. "Okay, 'nother question . . ."

"Sure, but just one." He smiles.

I'm tempted to ask him to the spring formal. But, being that it's just January, I know that would be premature. Besides, I'm crossing my fingers that he'll ask me first. Instead, I ask what's been on my mind since homeroom. "How'd you get so tan in Colorado?"

"A tanning bed."

I stop in midwalk and repeat, "A tanning bed?"

"Yeah. They had one at the resort. I had to even out the ski flush on my face. Everyone's gonna think I went to the beach."

Oh, no! I'm turned off for a second. I can't like a fake baker. Girls going tanning is fine . . . but guys? I have strict rules against liking metrosexuals. My theory is that no guy should take longer to get ready than I do. I try to sneak a peek at his eyebrows to see if he waxes them. This, indeed, is a huge deal breaker in my book. However, I don't get past the adorable glimmer in his green eyes. I fall deep into his stare and decide that I'll make a metrosexual exception for him regardless.

"This is my stop," I say, pointing to the locker room. I briefly forget the dragon wench named Britney Taylor who awaits me. Matt and I stand grinning at each other awkwardly. Should I hug him? Would that be cheesy, desperate, uncomfortable . . . or some other adjective that I can't think of while staring at his delicious lips?

As I'm contemplating my next move, my arch-nemesis emerges from the locker room in her disgustingly tight gym clothes. Like a vulture, she immediately spots us and begins to make her way over.

"Ewwww, Matt—don't waste your time with that lezza-saurus," Britney hisses, prancing toward us.

"Shut up," I retort, embarrassed that that's the best comeback I can think of.

She glares at me as she inches closer.

I immediately turn my attention to Matt to gauge his reaction. I can tell he's trying not to stare at her cantaloupe boobage. I instantly grow jealous.

"You should be with a real woman," she says enticingly with one hand on her hip and the other rubbing his chest.

His pupils dilate, and he gets a sleazy dirty-old-man type of a grin on his face. A major flirt festival is developing before my eyes. I'm more jealous than ever. I can't take it anymore!

"I'm sure Kyle would love to see this!" I snap.

Britney stops what she's doing and twirls around.

"Jealous much, April?" She snarls, sauntering past into the gymnasium.

I watch Matt's eyes tune in to her perky butt.

"You should get going, Matt; the bell's going to ring," I say, feeling defeated by a pair of melon boobs and a toned hind end.

Grrrrr. Once again, Britney has stolen my moment . . . and all I can think about is implementing the Lipstick Lawbreaker plan.

After stewing on my disdain for Britney for half of the day, by lunchtime I'm more than ready to begin our Lipstick Law-breaker plan to dethrone her.

"Today in gym, Ms. Hoops kicked Brit out of the volleyball game for aiming every serve at my head," I rehash as the girls and I sit down at our table.

Rachel claps. "Good for Ms. Hoops! I love that little lady!"

"And," I say, "Brit made another pass at Mr. Hottie-Body."

"She has nerve. Why does she think she can get any guy she wants?" Ashley complains.

" 'Cause no one's ever said no," Melanie explains.

"Except Troy Hoffman!" I remind them excitedly.

We all look at Ashley. "Did you bring the letter?"

"Of course! It's the only reason I wanted to come back to school today," she says, pulling the crisp sheet of paper from her bag. We all helped dictate the letter last week, and Ashley jumped at the chance to transcribe the fake Troy letter to paper.

The girls and I glance around suspiciously, making sure no spying eyes are on us. When the coast is clear, we hover around the letter guardedly:

> BRITNEY,
>
> I PROBABLY SHOULDN'T BE WRITING THIS, BUT I CAN'T HELP HOW I FEEL. YOU'RE ALWAYS ON MY MIND, AND I'M HOPING YOU FEEL THE SAME WAY ABOUT ME. I KNOW WE'RE BOTH IN RELATIONSHIPS RIGHT NOW, AND I DON'T WANT TO HURT ANYBODY, BUT I HAVE TO FOLLOW MY HEART. PLEASE LET ME KNOW IF YOU'RE INTERESTED IN ME. IF YOU ARE, AND WANT TO WRITE ME BACK, LEAVE YOUR REPLY IN LOCKER 223H. I'D LIKE TO KEEP THIS UNDER WRAPS FOR NOW, UNTIL WE FIGURE EVERYTHING OUT. I HOPE TO HEAR FROM YOU SOON. UNTIL THEN, I'LL BE THINKING OF YOU.
>
> LOVE,
> TROY (AKA HOFF)

I squirm excitedly on the plastic cafeteria chair. "Good job, Ashley! It really looks like a guy's handwriting!"

"Thanks. It's called chicken scratch." She laughs.

"His nickname at the end is perfect," Melanie adds.

"Do you think Britney will be able to keep her mouth shut about this letter? That could blow the whole thing for us if she doesn't," Rachel points out.

Melanie scans the letter again. "Troy's asking her to keep it under wraps, remember? She's obsessed with him. She'll do whatever he tells her."

Smirking, I say, "If that's the case, maybe Troy should ask her to jump off a bridge in his next letter."

Ashley nods, her brown eyes shining between her long eyelashes as she tucks the letter into a scented envelope. "Not a bad idea, Apes. I like that!"

"Is that cologne?" Melanie asks, sniffing the envelope.

Ashley nods. "I thought it was a nice touch."

"Definitely," Rachel says. "We should slip it in her locker now while we know where she is."

"Good idea," I agree. "Do you want to go while we all keep an eye on her here?"

"Sure, I'll be right back." Rachel grabs the envelope and dashes out of the cafeteria. We watch Britney and her followers from afar. We look away for a minute when we notice Erin pointing to our table.

"They're probably playing the Rank-a-Skank game," I say.

"Well, we know we're all a five on that scale now," Melanie replies with a shrug.

Ashley has class with Britney seventh period, and I can hardly wait for her to text me about it. First, however, I have to sit through Mr. Gonzales's lecture on Spanish pronouns. I catch Jessica looking at me; she smiles before I look away. Why is she acting so friendly lately? She has to be up to something.

When the bell rings, I rush to my science class. I'm excited for two reasons: one being Ashley's text . . . and the other being that I'm super curious to see if Delvin McGerk's makeover translates as well in person as it did on the Christmas card.

I put my cell on vibrate and shove it in my front pocket as I sit down. Delvin strolls into class soon after. Surprisingly, I have to admit, he's definitely looking better these days. I mean, he's no A-list actor, but more like an awkward, halfway-decent-looking stagehand. I only hope that his lopsided glasses are in a dumpster somewhere and not being worn by another fashion victim.

"Hi, April Bowers!"

Ah—yes. Same old Delvin.

"Hi," I reply unenthusiastically.

He stumbles on his untied shoes as he walks past my desk.

Halfway through class, my phone vibrates in my pocket. I wait until the teacher isn't looking to take a peek at Ashley's text:

> UR not gonna believe
> this. It's on her desk.
> She keeps reading it.
> LOL! I think she might
> B writing him bck now!

Slipping the phone into my bag, I look around, smiling triumphantly. She's fallen for it—hook, line, and sinker! Delvin meets my eyes as I scan the room. He waves with a cheesy smile from across the class. Oh, no . . . he thinks I'm smiling at him.

It doesn't surprise me when he follows closely behind me as we're leaving class. I try to dart from him, but a varsity line-backer from the Penford football team blocks my escape.

"Hey there," he attempts to say smoothly.

"Hey. Nice new look, McGerk," I say, trying to be nice.

"Y-You . . . noticed?" he stutters elatedly.

Of course I noticed; you got rid of ten pounds of metal from your teeth and Coke-bottle glasses the size of Detroit. In spite of the obvious, I decide to censor my response. "Yeah, I can hardly recognize you."

He laughs, sounding like a donkey giving birth. "Thanks, Miss April Bowers."

"Just call me April," I remind him for the three hundredth time.

"Right." He nods.

"Well, gotta go! Bye," I blurt, making a swift getaway around the corner, leaving him stuck behind the wide linebacker.

I'm dying throughout eighth period, wondering if Britney has left a reply letter in locker 223H yet. I obsessively examine my cell for texts until my teacher yells at me to put it away.

I finally get the text I've been waiting for when I'm walking to history class. This time it's from Rachel:

> Checked the ♥ locker &
> found letter.
> See U after school 2
> read it!

The four of us crowd into Melanie's car after school. Guarding the letter, Rachel says, "Let's go somewhere else to read it. I don't want anyone seeing it."

Mel drives to the gas station down the street, and Rachel reads Britney's response.

Troy,
   I was so happy to get your letter. You're on my mind all the time too! I always thought you had feelings for me. I can tell by the way you look at me. I know we'd make a much cuter couple than you and Jamie. You deserve a girl who's as hot as you are. Write back ASAP. I'll be waiting!
Love,
Brit

"Barfo!" Rachel exclaims, putting her finger down her throat as she finishes.

"She's so conceited!" Melanie fumes.

"It's no surprise that you love me; everyone does! I'm the hottest girl in the school, didn't you know? Write back ASAP. Love, Brit!" Ashley mimics in a bratty voice.

"Can I see it? She didn't even mention Kyle!" I gasp, reaching for her letter.

Later that evening, we have a Lipstick Lawbreaker meeting to create the next letter from fake Troy. We're bubbling with ideas.

"Maybe we should take this in a whole new direction and leave her a really mean note from Troy," Rachel says. "That'll devastate her!"

"No, no," I say. "If we stick it out with the love letters, the ending will be so much more rewarding."

"True," Rachel agrees. "I just hate feeding her ego."

Melanie scoffs. "Her ego is already fed by the air she breathes."

"I still like April's idea of having Troy suggest that she jump off a bridge," Ashley says nonchalantly while doodling in a notebook.

Eventually, we agree on a letter that (fingers crossed) will force Britney to talk crap about Jamie and Kyle:

> BRIT,
>
> I'M SO RELIEVED THAT YOU FEEL THE SAME WAY. JUST LIKE EVERY OTHER GUY IN THE SCHOOL, I'VE WANTED TO BE WITH YOU FOR A WHILE NOW. WE'D MAKE A HOT COUPLE. IT'S TOO BAD THAT WE'RE STUCK IN OUR RELATIONSHIPS. HOW SHOULD WE WORK AROUND THEM? DO YOU THINK I SHOULD BREAK UP WITH JAMIE? WOULD YOU BE WILLING TO BREAK UP WITH KYLE FOR ME? REMEMBER TO KEEP QUIET ABOUT EVERYTHING FOR NOW. IF I HAVE MY WAY, WE'LL BE TOGETHER SOON ENOUGH. I CAN'T WAIT TO HEAR BACK FROM YOU.
>
> LOVE,
> HOFF

It takes Britney a few periods to respond to the new letter the next day. We all gather in the school library to read it before heading to lunch.

Dear Hoff,

Of course you should dump Jamie! I've never liked her. No one does! No offense, but she's an undercover scag. Guys like you shouldn't be stuck with charity cases like her. As for Kyle, I don't want to be with him anymore, anyway. He's starting to annoy me. He'll just have to get over it. I promise this is our secret until the time is right. Write back soon.

Love,
Brit

We all look at each other with our mouths hanging open.

"Wow!" I say. "She let it all out!"

Rachel cackles. "Mwah-ha-ha-ha-ha! The sea of evidence is building up around her . . . Soon enough, she'll drown in it!"

"Kyle and Jamie are gonna be livid when they get their hands on this!" Mel squeals.

"We could probably close up shop right now with this letter," I say.

"And stop the fun?" Ashley grins. "No way!"

chapter fourteen

By mid-January, Britney and "Hoff" have exchanged twenty-five letters, give or take. She has completely word-butchered Jamie and Kyle like we had hoped, but we're getting worried, because she seems to be frustrated with Troy. This is especially evident in her most recent letter:

> *Hoff,*
>
> *I'm waiting on Kyle until you dump Jamie. Why haven't you gotten rid of her yet? Also, I don't know why you hardly acknowledge me when I try to talk to you. I'm not desperate, so stop acting like you have all the time in the world to make what we have together public! I'm sick of keeping this a secret. You need to figure things out soon, or I'll take your letters to Jamie myself. You have my number, so CALL me!*
> *—Brit*

"Look, she didn't use the *L* word at the end this time," Ashley points out.

Shaking my head, I say, "Told you guys we should've stopped when she wrote the letter saying Jamie's fat and Kyle's boring."

Melanie paces around my room nervously. "Okay, guys, we can't let her go to Jamie before we do," she says. "We'll have to make copies of her letters tonight and give them to Jamie and Kyle tomorrow."

We all nod in agreement.

"Girls, it's time to enforce Operation Destroy Britney Taylor!" I say. "This is what we've been waiting for . . ."

The next day, we go to school with a couple important packages in tow. We skip the first half of lunch to deliver them. First, we slip fake Troy's last letter to Britney in her locker.

> BRITNEY,
>   SORRY IT'S TAKEN ME SO LONG, BUT I'M READY TO GO PUBLIC WITH OUR RELATIONSHIP. IN FACT, I WANT TO PROFESS MY LOVE FOR YOU THIS AFTERNOON! MEET ME ON THE FOOTBALL FIELD AFTER SCHOOL. I DON'T CARE WHO SEES US — INVITE THE WHOLE SCHOOL IF YOU WANT. I CAN'T WAIT TO SEE YOU, BEAUTIFUL.
>   LOVE,
>   HOFF

Next, we drop the manila envelopes containing copies of Britney's incriminating letters into Jamie's and Kyle's lockers. Along with her letters, the envelopes also include a detailed explanation, an invitation to confront Britney this afternoon on the football field, and instructions to avoid her until then. If all goes well, she'll be waiting for Troy to profess his love when in reality, Jamie and Kyle will be professing their wrath.

He cringes with rage. "You can have Troy, Brit! You wanna know why?"

"Um . . . 'cause you can't stop me?"

He scoffs. "Nope! More like because I don't want your flat ass anymore! You're not half as great as you think you are!"

"Flat ass is right!" someone from the crowd jeers.

Rachel, Mel, Ashley, and I cover our mouths to choke back the giggles.

Kyle shakes his head and continues, "You're in for a big surprise! And don't come runnin' back to me when Troy disses you!"

"You wish," Brit mumbles conceitedly.

He turns to storm off and bellows, "She's all yours, Bradshaw, give 'er hell!"

Britney's eyes grow wide with dread when confronted with Jamie's death stare.

"Do these look familiar, Brit-brat?" Jamie points to the letters. Laughter at Britney's new nickname radiates through the crowd.

"Bradshaw is pissed!" a guy on the sideline yells with surprise. Jamie Bradshaw was voted friendliest in last year's yearbook. Everyone is shocked to see her looking so mad.

Britney backs up uncomfortably.

"So Britney, I'm fat, ugly, and an undercover scag? I'm a charity case, am I?"

Looking around nervously for support, Britney stutters, "I—I—I just—"

Jamie cuts her off mockingly. "You—you—you're just better than me, right?"

Brit, annoyed with Jamie's sarcasm, resumes her usual cocky stance and mutters, "Glad you're admitting it."

We're brimming with nerves and excitement once we've planted all of our evidence.

"Do you think Britney will fall for it?" Melanie asks, biting her lip.

"Of course she will; her arrogance won't allow her to think this is a prank," Rachel says confidently.

We all look at each other, smiling spitefully as we walk to the cafeteria to finish out the rest of lunch.

By ninth period, my palms are sweaty and my heart is racing like crazy. Ashley's seventh-period text had been really promising:

> Brit is digging her own grave. She's telling every1 2 come 2 the football field after school! She's making it sound like some big event is gonna go down. LOL!

But I'm still really nervous that things might go wrong. I prepare myself when the final bell rings. Fear sizzles in my throat as I make my way out into the jam-packed hallway. Everyone's bustling with gossip. Britney's random invites have erupted into curious rumors spreading rapidly throughout the halls.

"It's a surprise concert. I've seen them do that on MTV."

"I bet Mr. Stuart's having a satanic ritual out there."

"It's a fight. No doubt."

"It's probably just a senior prank."

"I heard someone's blowing up a junker car out there."

I quickly pass through all the rumors and meet the girls at Melanie's locker. The four of us file out the parking lot doors with a bunch of anxious schoolmates. The cold winter air takes my breath away as we walk toward the football field. Our shoes leave trails through the thin dust of snow covering the parking lot. There's already a large group of people gathered on the sideline. Britney's big mouth has made the prospect of spying easy for us. We merge into the middle of the students, crossing our fingers for a fantastic show.

"I don't see her." My warm breath dawdles through the chilly air.

"There she is!" Melanie points to a blonde in the middle of the endless stream of curious students making their way to the field.

"She's armored with the Lipstick Lawlords," Rachel says as Britney reaches the field surrounded by Erin, Brianna, and Jessica. Britney shoos her loyal followers to join the mob of onlookers and walks to the center of the field. The girls and I creep farther into the mix, to ensure that we won't be spotted by Brit or her Lawlord crew.

Looking eager, Britney tugs her Burberry scarf back and forth while scanning the mob for her Prince Charming. She smiles at the crowd, seemingly pleased with the large turnout.

"Aw—how sweet! You're all here for me?" She giggles, waving like a princess acknowledging peons.

"If things go as planned, she won't be smiling for too much longer," Ashley whispers to us.

The swarm of observers chatters.

"What's Britney Taylor doing out there?"

"Is she the show?"

"Maybe she's gonna *strip!*"

A group of meatheads begin to cheer, "Take it off! Take it off!"

Britney shoots them a dirty look. "Settle down, boys; Troy's not going to like that."

Within minutes, I spot Kyle and Jamie making their way to the field, camouflaged by straggling students.

"Look!" I point excitedly. "They're coming! And it looks like they're holding the letters!"

I can hardly contain myself when Britney notices them approaching. Her wide smile slowly disintegrates as they march closer and closer, looking furious.

Kyle strides up to her with his body rigid with anger and his eyebrows furrowed.

"I'm boring?" he growls. "Not as hot as Troy? The only good thing I have going for me is my parents' money?"

Britney stares at him like a deer in headlights.

The girls and I try to hold back laughter. The rest of the audience grows silent, anticipating the drama.

He moves closer to her. "You think I'm annoying, do you?"

She rolls her eyes and looks away.

"You want Troy?" he shouts, throwing the letters above her like confetti.

She brushes her hair off and snaps, "God, Kyle! You're such a girl. Get over it!"

The mob absorbs the drama with quiet gasps and whispers. Melanie grabs my hand, squeezing it firmly.

"You bitch!" Jamie explodes.

"Jamie, don't hate me because your boyfriend wants me," Britney taunts, curling her long locks around her manicured finger.

"Troy wants you? It's more like you want him!" Jamie circles around her, irate. "And, news flash, you're not gonna get him."

"Just deal with it, Jamie! He wants to dump you. I'm surprised he hasn't already," Britney says.

"Dump me for you?" Jamie laughs. "Troy thinks you're a whining, stuck-up little brat!"

Britney looks at her nail beds nonchalantly. "Right, Jamie, don't you wish?"

"Wish it? I know it! Who's the one that's dated him for two years?"

Britney rolls her eyes. "Not for much longer. He'd rather be with me."

"Who here would rather date Brit-brat Taylor over me?" Jamie asks the mobbed audience.

Silence.

Britney glares at her Lipstick Law followers with disapproval. "Thanks for the *support*, guys!" she shrieks, sending them into a panicked frenzy. She turns back to Jamie, pointing at the pack of letters she's gripping. "Don't ask the crowd, ask Troy! It shouldn't be a surprise to you . . . Obviously you read our letters!"

Jamie shoves the letters in her face. "Don't you realize this isn't even Troy's handwriting? You're such an idiot! Someone made a fool of you!"

The crowd laughs.

"Yes, it is!" Britney insists, grabbing the letters.

"Read them all you want," Jamie hisses while pulling out a water bottle from her bag. "You wouldn't know what his hand-writing looks like because you've never seen it!"

The color drains from Britney's face as she begins to doubt the authenticity of the letters. While she inspects them fever-ishly, Jamie inches closer to her, twisting the cap off of the bot-tle of water.

"Since you think you're so hot . . . I'd like to help you cool down," she announces, dumping the water over Britney's head.

Brit lets out a bloodcurdling scream. She immediately throws a toddler tantrum in the middle of the field, ripping the letters into shreds and screeching like a maniac. Her loyal fol-lowers run to console her while Jamie struts away victoriously. Ironically, the large crowd Britney enticed to the field has turned on her, heckling hysterically.

My mouth drops open; the girls and I jump up and down excitedly—trying not to miss the action over the riled-up crowd around us. This has gone better than any of us could have ever imagined.

"I'm soaking wet! Get me a towel!" Britney screams, spitting water from her lips. Brianna takes off her Fendi scarf and sur-renders it to wipe off Brit's dripping wet hair and jacket. She immediately stains it with the dark eye makeup that's running down her face.

Britney's attention quickly pans to the once welcome crowd watching her embarrassing display from the side of the field. "What are you jackasses looking at?"

"A wet rat!" someone calls out from the middle of the group.

Someone else yells, "An ugly, wet Brit-brat rat!"

The crowd bursts into laughter. Britney's big brown eyes swell with wrath. The girls and I laugh so hard, we have to huddle together to keep each other from falling down.

Seething, Britney stomps up to the parking lot, with her trusty followers scrambling behind her. Her mouth drops in horror as she watches Jamie climb into Troy's truck.

Troy rolls down the window and yells, "In your dreams, Taylor!"

Britney kicks a small patch of snow at the truck as it speeds away. "I never wanted you anyway! You'll be bald by thirty!" She then turns to Erin and yells, "Don't just stand there like an orange dolt! Get your car, and let's get the hell out of here!"

chapter fifteen

Even though the fake Troy sting couldn't have gone any better on the football field a couple weeks ago, and half the school is shunning Brit-brat Taylor like the plague, the girls and I are just a tad let down that no one's figured out that it was our genius plan behind the chaos.

"I can't believe she doesn't even suspect us," I say, disappointed as we browse at Eastview Mall.

"Why are you surprised? She has the brain of a marshmallow," Ashley says.

"A melted marshmallow," Rachel adds.

"Speaking of marshmallows, look! It's five-for-three at Mrs. Fields!" Melanie points to the cookie nook.

"Craving sugar again, Mel?" I say, referring to Mel's undying sweet tooth.

She joins the short line of fellow cookie-cravers and smiles back at me. "What can I say? TOM is in town."

We follow her to the sugar haven.

"That creeper drives you to sugar rampages every month," Ashley says.

"Periods suck . . . period," Mel says, inspecting the delicious morsels behind the glass counter.

I change the subject. "Hey, Ashley, does Britney still think it was Brandon Smith?"

"As far as I can tell. She thinks Brandon didn't want Kyle

dating her anymore. I guess she and Brandon got in an argument shortly before the first fake Troy letter appeared. I overheard her telling Erin that she'd like to strangle him in his sleep."

We shake our heads in disbelief.

"Brandon has a hard enough time passing his classes; he could never pull off an elaborate hoax like that," Rachel says.

"I almost want to tell her," Melanie says after placing her cookie order.

"I know," I agree. "Half the fun of pulling something like that off is taking credit for it afterward."

"And getting the praise," Ashley adds. "I mean, we made dreams come true for countless Brat-ney Taylor haters!"

"And there are millions of them," I confirm.

Melanie peers into her cookie buffet bag happily.

"You going to share?" we ask.

"Of course, but I get two."

"Remember Lipstick Law Three, Melanie! You better watch it!" Ashley teases, flipping her long dark hair like Britney. Her shiny highlights reflect the lighting above.

Mel laughs. "If I were still following those, I would've been kicked out four pounds ago."

"If we were still following those, we'd be in strict violation of our MPOA right now," I say, pointing to the "restricted" food court area.

By the middle of February, we decide that we have to take credit where credit is due. The school has been buzzing over who was behind the Britney Taylor freak show . . . and we can't let Brandon bask in the glory any longer.

We begin our admission-of-guilt plan by purchasing a sympathy card that reads:

When times of sorrow fall upon good people like you,
know that you can depend on your friends
to help get you through.

We scribble out the words *good* and *friends* and replace them with STUCK-UP and LIPSTICK LAWS. The girls and I gather in my bedroom, where our midnight black lipstick emerges from hiding after a short hibernation period. The four of us giggle deviously as we sign the card under its text with our Lipstick Lawbreaker smooches. Ashley pens a nice note in fake Troy's handwriting on the blank side of the card, opposite our kisses:

DEAREST BRIT-BRAT,
WE'RE SO SORRY THINGS DIDN'T WORK OUT
BETWEEN YOU AND HOFF. YOU MAY NOT HAVE HIM,
BUT REMEMBER, YOU'LL ALWAYS HAVE THE
LIPSTICK LAWS!
    KISSES,
    THE LIPSTICK LAWBREAKERS

"I wish I could see her face when she reads this," Melanie says as we approach her locker to make our confession deposit.

Rachel reaches the card to the top of Britney's locker. She hesitates before taking the plunge. "This might start a Lipstick war."

The rest of us assert, "Do it!"

She slips the card into the locker vent, which we've found doubles as a perfect mail slot. We prepare for battle the rest of our lunch period.

⁂

In the middle of Spanish class, I notice Jessica reading a text on her cell. She gasps loudly, making Señor Gonzales jump at the chalkboard.

"*Problemo,* Jessica?" he asks.

"No . . . no, Señor."

She looks over at me when he turns back around. I smile at her.

She mouths, "Did you?"

I know what she's talking about, yet I can't help but pretend that I don't understand. "What?" I mouth dramatically.

She whispers, "Did you set Brit up?"

"Set Brit up?" I shrug my shoulders, looking confused.

She rolls her eyes and mutters softly, "You know what I'm talking about."

Shaking my head, I whisper, *"No comprendo . . ."*

Once class is over, Jessica follows me out to confront me in the hallway.

"Were you behind the Troy letters?"

"Me? Behind them? No. In front of them . . . well, that's a different story," I say sarcastically.

"Did you set up the whole football field episode too?" she asks with her hand perched aggressively on her size zero hip.

"Did Britney put tampons on my locker and a huge hole in the crotch of my favorite jeans?" I say back curtly.

She stares at me quizzically, tucking her shiny black hair behind her ears.

"The answer's yes," I admit. "But I wasn't the only one."

"Melanie Elmer?" Jessica inquires with narrowed eyes.

"Ashley Mitchell and Rachel Johnson, too. We mustn't forget them," I say in a patronizing tone, looking down on her domineeringly.

Jessica looks completely stunned. Her golden glow turns pale. Slipping her hands into the pockets of her True Religion jeans, she rocks her petite body to and fro. She looks around nervously, as if she doesn't know who to trust anymore.

"What?" I say. "You Lipstick Lawlords didn't think we could pull something like that off?"

"I just . . . I just," she utters quietly.

I'm amused by her speechlessness.

"You just what?"

Her dark eyes pan up and down over me, clearly reevaluating my aptitude. "I just thought you were too nice to do something like that."

"Too nice?" I repeat, put off by her response.

"Well, yeah. You always seemed nice . . . all of you," she reiterates.

Is she mocking me or being sincere? I can't tell, and it's aggravating me.

I glower. "If you thought we were so nice, why didn't you side with us in the first place?"

"Because . . ." She pauses, looking down. "Well, I don't know."

"Don't talk to me again until you figure that out, Jessica!" I say, walking away briskly.

Within a couple weeks, the majority of appreciative classmates have affectionately crowned us the Con Queens, which Melanie insists is a much more prestigious title than prom queen. Our newfound popularity comes as a surprise, mainly because I never realized just how many people detested Britney Taylor. I mean, I always knew she was loathed by a decent amount of people . . . but I had no clue that the Brat-ney Taylor hate club was swarming with members. The girls and I have been immersed with thank-yous, rounds of standing applause, and genuine butt-kissing. We're suddenly propelled out of the misfit-dom that the Lipstick Laws tried to sentence us to. The one person that I care about, however, has a different perspective.

"I just think it's all pretty shady." Matt frowns as we poke our way through the jammed hallway.

I study his face to see if he's joking. He's not.

"Matt, you just don't understand—she's evil! She totally deserved it!"

"She's not evil, April . . . but even so, what about the others?" he asks.

"What others?"

"Like Kyle, Troy, and Jamie. Those others."

"Oh. Ummm . . . what about them?" I say.

"Well, did you guys think about what they'd think of all this?"

I bite my lip apprehensively.

"I don't mean to put a damper on your new royal status," he says. "But I'm sure it had to suck for them."

"Ummm . . ." I pause, considering the fact that he definitely has a point. Feeling bad, I say, "Well, no . . . I guess we didn't really think about that."

I wrinkle my face into a nonverbal *oops*. I feel his disapproving eyes sucking out my sinful soul.

"But, I'm sure they don't mind." I try to minimize the situation. "It was the only way to show her true colors. They're probably thankful like the rest of the school."

I look at him for some reassurance. Instead, I'm suckerpunched with silence. I have a nagging feeling that this means he won't be asking me to the spring formal anytime soon.

"I talked to Kyle yesterday," I fib. "He thanked me."

"As long as you're cool with it," Matt says cynically as we part for class.

Crap, is he siding with Brat-ney? This isn't good.

Several students salute and bow to me when I enter the classroom. I smile awkwardly as I sit down at my art table. Sure, the Lipstick Lawbreakers may be hailed as underdog heroes now, but what good is that if I can't share our success with Mr. Hottie-Body Brentwood? I can barely concentrate throughout class.

Mrs. Duffy makes me an example, commenting on my use of dark paint colors and jerky hand movements. "See, class, painting can be great therapy!"

Later that night I call Haley. She was more than delighted to find out how successful our Lipstick Lawbreaker plan had been, and has insisted on being given regular updates since. Of course, I immediately tell her about my weird conversation with Matt today.

"Do you think he likes her?"

"I don't know. It kind of seemed that way," I say gloomily.

"Why would he be concerned with Troy, Jamie, and Kyle? He's not friends with them, is he?"

"No, it's like he was trying to make me feel guilty . . . and it worked. He's probably working for Britney now. I bet she hypnotized him with her large chestoid," I grumble, blowing a curl from my face.

"I don't think you have to worry about that. Large chestoids are overrated."

"Not to Matt," I refute. "He seems captivated by her melon boobs whenever he sees her."

"Ick! He sounds like a dirtbag. If that's the case, you shouldn't want him anyhow," she says.

I know she's right, but he's too hot not to like.

She promptly changes the subject, aware that boobage is a sore spot of mine. "Any new incidents I should know about?"

"Other than throwing gum in my hair in gym class yesterday and tripping Ashley when she walked to the front of her class for a speech this week, she's been lying low for the most part."

"Hmmm . . . that seems pretty bleak on the Brit Taylor scale of evil doings," Haley points out.

"I know. It's sort of weird, but I feel like the whole Troy Hoffman hoopla deflated her ego a little."

"Not possible!" Haley disagrees. "She's probably just scheming."

"I'm sure you're right, Lee. I shouldn't underestimate her evilness."

"So, did you get the gum out of your hair?"

"Mel helped me cut a big chunk out. You can hardly tell because of my curls. This is the one time in my life that I've been thankful for my crazy head of hair."

"I love your curls," Haley says enviously. I could argue with her (as usual) for days about how I'd die to have her hair. Hair that doesn't frizz into a rat's nest in humid weather . . . hair that dries out of the shower perfectly straight . . . hair that I could pull back in a ponytail without worrying that it'll get snarled around the band . . . thick, beautiful straight-as-a-board hair. Instead, I glance down at my Kleenex boob buds and mull over why God gave me curves growing out of my head instead of my chest.

Haley breaks the silence. "Apes?"

"Yeah . . . thanks, Lee, but you know how I feel about my hair. "

"You're crazy," she says before changing the subject. "Anyway, someone's birthday is coming up soon! Is that someone excited?"

"It should be fun." I try to sound happy. After all, I should be excited for my sixteenth birthday, but I'm not. I had pictured Matt and I dating by the time the month of April popped up. On the contrary, the whole idea of being his girlfriend seems to be getting more and more far-fetched as time goes on.

"Maybe if you're lucky," Haley hints, "you'll be getting a big surprise!"

I smile, daydreaming that my big surprise will be a Mr. Hottie-Body Brentwood wrapped in a bow.

That night I have another nightmare. Jamie, Kyle, and Troy are lying unresponsive in hospital beds. Black lipstick is smeared on their faces. The doctor comes in, looking at his clipboard, shaking his head.

"The prognosis is bad," he says grimly.

Alarm surges through my body. "How bad?"

"They're not going to make it."

Sobbing, I rush to the doctor for a shoulder to cry on. He brushes me away like a pesky fly, revealing his stern face. He's Matt Brentwood!

"It's all your fault, April. Look what you've done!" Matt reprimands.

Just then, Britney Taylor struts into the room dressed like a sexy police officer. She dangles handcuffs in front of me. Wincing, I reluctantly put my wrists out to be cuffed.

She laughs at me and says, "These aren't for you. They're for Dr. Hottie-Body. We're bound to have some fun with them!"

I wake up, horrified beyond belief, as they start kissing.

chapter sixteen

I've spent the last month concentrating on redeeming my nice-girl image with Matt Brentwood. Hurling all my efforts into winning him over almost makes me forget that it's the start of my birthday weekend. It's Friday night, and my family whisks me away to a celebratory dinner at my favorite Italian restaurant in East Rochester. I get the tortellini alfredo. It's to die for. Technically, I guess it really could be to die for . . . hence my father's nickname for it: heart attack on a plate. Regardless of its artery-clogging qualities, it's delicious!

On the car ride home, my parents are acting super suspicious . . . and my brother keeps staring at me with a goofy I-know-something-you-don't smile. I pray that they're not planning a surprise party, like the one I wet my pants at when I turned ten. All those kids jumping out screaming "Surprise!" scared the hell out of me . . . or, scared the pee out of me is more like it. Seeing that I just drank four Diet Cokes at dinner, my bladder would probably go berserk if prompted by party hats and Silly String again.

"What's Mel's car doing here?" I ask warily as we pull up to the driveway. "She's not supposed to be here until tomorrow night."

My mom glances at my dad with a dubious smile. "She offered to pick up the cake."

"I hope you remember that I hate surprises," I warn.

"Don't worry, Peebody, you won't be flooding your pants this year." My brother laughs. He called me this relentlessly for a year after the dreadful surprise party incident, and I'm less than thrilled to hear the nickname come out of retirement.

"Be nice, Aaden. It's her sweet sixteenth, and sweet it should be!" my dad scolds, putting the car in park beside Mel's white Ford Taurus.

I'm relieved when I'm greeted by Melanie—and Melanie alone—at the door. She gives me a big hug. "Long time no see! Happy birthday, chica!"

"Thanks! Did you do this?" I point to the streamers and birthday decorations adorning the front hallway.

"Maybe," she says with a smile. "Your 'rents bought everything. I just worked my decorating magic while you chowed down on Italian food."

Melanie had gone out of her way to make my day extra special at school, too. Walking up to the colorful happy birthday banner she made for my locker was an amazing reminder of just how far I've come from the tampon graffiti days. She and the girls even presented me with a cookie cake at lunch. They provoked half of the cafeteria to help them sing "Happy Birthday" to me. Of course, that half of the cafeteria didn't include the Lipstick Lawlords. However, that half of the cafeteria did include Mr. Hottie-Body Brentwood . . . and that's all that counts!

We proceed into the dining room. A pink, glittery sweet sixteen sign is hanging from the chandelier. It eerily reminds me of Britney's drag queen bedroom. My mom picks up a small box wrapped in girly pink and white flowered paper from the pile of gifts.

She hands it to me and says, "This one first."

"Car keys?" I wink slyly.

My dad laughs sarcastically. "Right."

"Don't get ahead of yourself. You don't even have your license yet, April," my mom reminds me.

"Okay, so I get the car after I get my license?"

She looks at my dad and protests, "Your father and I never had cars in high school."

Aaden crosses his arms defiantly. "That's because cars didn't exist back then!"

I laugh. I've heard this argument ever since my brother got his license last year. Apparently, he's sick of tagging along with Jeffrey Higgins. Jeffrey's goat laugh is probably getting to him.

I go ahead and open the small present only to find a note inside.

"Aw, how thoughtful," I say. "A treasure hunt!"

The only other time my parents set up a birthday present treasure hunt was for my sixth birthday. They hid the bike I wanted in the storage shed outside. The giant purple bow that decorated the handlebars stayed on my head for the rest of the day.

"Well . . . read it, Bean," my dad says.

I hold the clue up and clear my throat playfully before reading. "Go to the place where you lay your head. You'll find your next clue under your"—I fill in the blank as I rush up the stairs—"bed!"

I peek under my bed and grab the second box. I open it quickly to reveal the next clue.

"Now go down the hall to your sacred room. Your next clue is where you choose to groom."

I dash to the bathroom and look in the towel chest, tub, and tissue box. Finally, I find the third wrapped box in the cabinet under the sink, next to my wild mane supplies.

"You're getting closer; just two more clues. Look for your next hint where you keep your . . . shoes?" I blurt as I run to my closet, finding a box tucked in a sneaker.

"You'll find your last clue somewhere downstairs—tucked in Dad's favorite chair." This fourth clue leads me to the re-cliner in the family room. I find the box wedged between the arm and the cushion and rip it open.

"Go to the room that's underground. That's where your present will be found!" I read slowly.

Looking at my parents, I ask, "The game room?"

My mom shrugs with a smile. "I don't know; you'll have to check it out."

My family and Mel follow me to the basement door. A bolt of anxiety hits me as I turn the lights on to walk down the stairs. I'm praying that no one jumps out at me screaming, "Surprise!" I picture myself tumbling down the stairs like a slinky after a horde of bratty kids spray Silly String in my face.

I close my eyes to protect them as I reach the bottom step.

It's cold . . . cold and quiet. The only sound I hear is Aaden snickering at the top of the stairs. I open one eye slowly to find an empty game room. I look back at my parents curiously.

"Take a look around, April," they prompt me.

Melanie nods excitedly.

I walk cautiously around the pool table. I look under it, and then I make my way to the bar area. As soon as I step past the bar stools, someone comes flying out from behind the couch across the room, scaring me to bits.

I cover my head like I'm practicing a bomb drill.

Everyone laughs. Then, I hear a familiar voice . . .

"Happy birthday, Apes!"

"Lee!" I shout, jumping to tackle her with a bear hug. "How'd you get here?"

She giggles. "Told you you'd have a big surprise on your birthday. I wasn't lying!"

After jumping around excitedly for a good five minutes, I am drawn to the pendant around her neck. I had given her the star necklace before she moved. Her goal is to one day have a star on Hollywood Boulevard, so until then, I figured she should wear one around her neck. Haley promised not to take it off until she becomes an actual Hollywood starlet.

"You're wearing the necklace I gave you!"

Smiling, Haley grabs the silver charm and nods. "Of course, I promised."

I'm completely giddy as I open my other presents and blow out my birthday candles. I haven't seen Haley in nearly nine months, and she looks almost the same . . . except for her new haircut. I guess she decided to bite the bullet and cut her long locks into a posh bob like she always said she would. I never believed she'd do it . . . but I'm glad to be proven wrong in person.

As my birthday activities wind down, my family dwindles off into separate rooms and Melanie goes home to let me and Haley catch up.

"I really like her," Haley says after Mel leaves. "I got to hang out with her when you guys were at dinner."

"She's awesome," I say. "When you become a celebrity, she can be your marriage therapist."

"Huh?"

"Never mind." I smile. "She's great. I couldn't have gotten through the whole Lipstick Laws mess without her."

"Can I see it?" Haley's amber eyes glisten. "Can I see the Oath?"

I pull the Lipstick Lawbreaker Oath out of my nightstand drawer, handing it to her with a big grin. "You wanna add your pucker pout to it?"

"I can't, can I?"

"Of course! You're a Lipstick Lawbreaker, aren't you?"

"Well, yeah."

"Actually Lee, you're one of our founders. You gave me the idea," I say, grabbing the midnight black lipstick from my makeup drawer.

"I'd be honored," she says with a cheesy grin.

I laugh, handing her the lipstick.

After adding her morbid lipstick stamp to the oath, her face lights up. "How could I forget? I have another surprise for you!"

She heads to her suitcase, lying in front of my closet door, and opens it. I don't know what could possibly surprise me more than her visit.

"You'll probably have to get the wrinkles steamed out of it," she cautions as she sorts through her clothes.

I kneel beside her inquisitively. "What is it?"

"Close your eyes!"

"They're closed," I say, shutting them tightly. A cool breeze passes my face when she stands up beside me.

"Okay, open 'em!" Haley orders.

I open my eyes and see her whirling around my room holding the most gorgeous, flowing lavender dress.

"Your favorite color!" Haley sings. "Do you love it?"

I bounce to my feet to get a closer look. "I love it! It's beautiful!"

"Well . . . it's yours!"

"No way!" I blurt.

"Yes way!" she says. "It's authentic Oscar de la Renta. The best part is, it's been on the red carpet."

"Hollywood?" I pant.

"Yep! Jessica Alba! Can you believe it?"

"But—but," I stammer, "How'd you—"

"Tessa got it for me."

I've always wanted to meet Tessa. She's Haley's fabulously glamorous cousin. She moved to Hollywood to become an actress, but found celebrity styling to be more interesting. Haley's hoping that one day Tessa will take her under her wing to show her the ropes of Tinseltown.

I'm feeling exhilarated, so I take a seat on my bed. "I can't keep this, Lee. It's too nice."

"Of course you can. It's your present!"

"But, don't you want it?" I ask.

"Tessa will get me one some other time. Besides, since Jordan and I split, I don't even want to think about *my* sophomore dance."

"Dance?" I repeat unenthusiastically.

She cocks her head to the side, looking concerned. "Well, yeah . . . that's where I pictured you wearing it. At Penford's spring formal."

"Haley, thank you so much. It's amazing. I love it. I really do! But I don't think it will be making an appearance at the spring formal this year."

She sits down next to me. "Why?"

"For starters, no one's asked me."

"Why don't you take initiative and ask Matt? It's the twenty-first century, girl, get with the program!" she says.

"I don't know," I mumble apprehensively. "I was hoping he'd ask me, but I don't think it will happen at this point. And I don't have the guts to ask him, that's for sure."

"C'mon, April, how many people have to tell you you're gorgeous before you start believing it? He'd be lucky to go with you. Maybe he's waiting for you to ask him."

"Nah." I shake my head bashfully.

"Whatever," she says. "You know he'll die when he sees you in this dress."

"Yeah, but . . ."

"No buts—you guys have been flirting since the first day of school. Just do it!"

"Maybe," I say, fidgeting nervously with a button on my shirt.

"Do the other girls have dates yet?"

I roll my eyes. "Of course. Ashley and Rachel are taking a couple guys they've known for a while. Two hotties from Fairfield High School."

"Oh—yummy!" Haley says. "Fairfield boys are the best."

I continue, "And Mark Rhinehart asked Mel last week."

"Mark Rhinehart?" Haley chokes. "That's totally random!"

"She thinks he's interesting . . . and she says they can share clothing," I explain.

Haley scrunches her nose like she always does when she's confused. "Since when does Melanie wear men's clothing?"

"No, no." I laugh. "Oh my gosh! I didn't tell you!"

"What?" Haley inches closer.

"Mark's an undercover cross-dresser!" I spit out in laughter.

"No way! Stop it!" Haley smacks my arm. "You're joking!"

"I wish I were!" I giggle, holding my stomach. "It's a long story. Let's not get into it."

"Ummmm . . . okay. Fascinating!" She laughs. "Well, he should make for a fun and fashionable date."

I nod, still laughing. "I think Melanie felt bad . . . so she said yes. She's too nice sometimes."

"Well, if she can go to the formal with an undercover cross-dresser, you should be able to get the nerve up to ask Mr. Hottie-Body," Haley insists.

"You might have a point." I giggle.

Haley grabs the Lipstick Lawbreaker Oath, putting her right hand up in the air.

"Put your hand up and repeat after me," she demands.

I put my right hand up reluctantly.

"I, April Bowers . . ."

"I, April Bowers," I repeat, half giggling.

"This is serious, Apes!" She continues, "Promise on the holy Lipstick Lawbreaker Oath to ask Mr. Hottie-Body Brentwood to the spring formal."

I take a few deep breaths. I haven't even had a date with Matt. How am I going to ask him out for the biggest night of the year? Not to mention, he's been so flippant with our flirting lately that I can't even tell if he likes me at all.

"C'mon, April," Haley prods.

"Er . . ." I glance at the beautiful dress she brought me and give in. "Fine. I promise on the Lipstick Lawbreaker Oath that I'll ask him to the spring formal."

Haley bursts out clapping, and I blush, feeling rejected by him already.

chapter seventeen

Saying goodbye to Haley at the airport on Sunday night is super sad. I'll miss her like crazy. She's like the sister I've never had . . . and the other girls love her, too. She fits in perfectly to our Lipstick Lawbreaker clique—which, I guess, makes perfect sense, seeing that she's the original Lawbreaker.

As I'm hugging her goodbye, she whispers in my ear, "Don't let that dress go to waste."

I squeeze her tightly and whisper back, "I won't."

"Promise me you'll ask him." She smiles, twisting her silver star necklace.

"I promise, Haley. I swore on the Oath."

Although I'm really sad to see her go, surprisingly, I don't cry this time. I bawled my eyes out the day she moved to Kansas. That was when she left me with no friends and an empty heart. This time, she's leaving me with three good friends and a heart that beats wildly for Mr. Hottie-Body Brentwood.

My heart is thudding throughout Mr. Stuart's attendance call . . . and this time it's not because of his monster truck body and booming voice. I glance at Matt out of the corner of my eye. This makes my heart pound even louder. I've never asked a guy out before . . . Well, at least not since Bobby Brynmar in second grade. His rejection morphed me into elementary hermit-hood for nearly three months. But I can't think about that now. I have to think happy thoughts . . . thoughts that will enhance my inner seductress. Thoughts like Mr. Hottie-Body on a—

"Scooter!" Mr. Stuart sneers. "What did I tell you about that crap in your mouth?"

He stomps to the varsity football jock in the back of homeroom. Holding out a Styrofoam cup, he orders, "Spit!"

I watch as Ryan "Scooter" Bryce spews out a chunky wad of dark brown nastiness. Mr. Stuart holds the cup in place for the remaining speckled saliva that's hanging from Scooter's lips to slowly ooze into the cup.

"And if anyone else decides that chewin' tobacco is cool," he barks, "I'm going to introduce you to my chinless uncle Steve!"

The class quivers in terror as he shakes the floor with his heavy walk back to the front desk. I hear my brother gulp from a few rows back. I can recognize his gulp from anywhere, as it's the same gulp he's gulped every time he's been caught in a lie—which, it turns out, is pretty often. While everyone else is cowering in fear, I smile. I'm pretty sure that I'm the only one who knows Mr. Stuart was once a football.

I'm shaking with nerves as I walk with Matt down the hallway. I know he can sense I'm nervous . . . which makes me even more nervous.

"Somethin' up?" he asks, giving a curious expression that's completely adorable.

I gander up at the ceiling; trying to be witty, I say, "Just the ugly fluorescent lights."

I soon realize this wasn't a witty joke at all. In fact, it may be one of the cheesiest things I've ever said. If I were close enough to a locker, I'd slam my head against it to punish myself for stupidity.

Matt looks at me, smiling; I laugh awkwardly.

"Really, April, you're acting different."

"Different?" I say, as if I don't know what he's referring to, even though I feel myself sweating incessantly.

He shakes his head. "I dunno, maybe it's just me . . . didn't get much sleep last night."

"Late night studying?" I question hopefully.

"Nope, wasn't studying."

Immediately, I grow suspicious over his reply. Who was he with, and where can I find her to chop her head off?

"So," I say, trying to hide my jealousy, "what were you doin' up so late?"

"Oh—I was on the phone . . . lost track of time."

"Interesting," I say, grinding my teeth. I pray that he was talking to one of his soccer buddies.

Remembering my promise to Haley, I try to refocus. "So . . . the spring formal's coming up in May."

"Yeah," he says. "Have any plans yet?"

Is Matt Brentwood asking *me* to the spring formal? Excitedly, I blurt, "Nope! Not yet!"

Did I make myself look too desperate?

"No?" he says with a puzzled expression that I'm not quite sure how to read.

I shake my head and ask, "How 'bout you? Do you have plans?"

"Yeah," he replies.

Yeah? What kind of an answer is "yeah"? My heart sinks to my knees. Does this mean he already has a date? Where do I go from here?

"What d'ya mean?"

He looks down guiltily. "Brit asked me yesterday."

Brit-brat? Suddenly, I realize that Britney Taylor was probably the one he was talking with on the phone last night. I can't conceal the hideous snarl on my face.

Seemingly concerned, he says, "I thought you already had a date. I'm sorry. You're not going to be mad at me, are you?"

"Yes!" I blurt, not meaning to. "I mean"—I force a laugh—"no . . . no . . . that's cool. I *do* already have a date."

He raises an eyebrow. "But . . . you just said—"

I cut him off, unable to control my agitated tone. "I just said I don't have plans yet. I didn't say I don't have a date. There's a big difference, Matt!"

❧

I stomp into the locker room with eyes like missiles. Marching to Britney's gym locker, ready to pummel her with my not-so-strong punch, I bite my hand in frustration when I see she's not there. I storm to my locker.

"Where is she?" I question Nancy, my gym partner.

She jumps, flinging her glasses halfway off her face.

"Who?" she asks, readjusting her specs.

"Britney Taylor!" I growl.

"Uh . . . I don't know." She backs up. Her hands are strangling a pair of fungus-ridden gym socks to death.

I realize I've approached poor Nancy like the Incredible Hulk, and try to regain my composure. "Did you see her?"

She squints her beady eyes, probably checking to see if my skin is turning green. "Um, no. But . . . she's probably already out there."

She points toward the door to the gymnasium.

I quickly change into my gym clothes, adding shin guards and elbow pads that we're required to wear for soccer. We're not practicing soccer in gym right now, but I plan on dribbling Britney's head like a soccerball, so I might as well dress the part.

Zipping into the gymnasium, I hurdle past a group of girls to get to the blond bimbo. I barely recognize her from behind because she's wearing a baggy sweatshirt . . . which is *so* against Lipstick Law Two, I can hardly believe my eyes.

I tap her on the shoulder. She turns around with a gasp. Clearly, the look on my face means business and she knows it. Her surprise turns into a patronizing smile. "Hey, April! What a co-inky-dink . . . We were just talking about you!"

The group of girls giggle beside her.

I point to her stomach. "What's with the sweatshirt, Brit? Looking pleasantly plump these days! Are you expecting, or have you been breaking Lipstick Law Three?" I spit out, "And aren't you violating Lipstick Law Two right now by wearing that?"

The girls around her whisper among themselves in disbelief. Their attention turns to Britney to see how she's going to react to my insults. Unfortunately, it doesn't bother her nearly as much as I expected.

Britney rolls her eyes at me. "Gym clothes don't count, scag. I was just waiting for you to get here to reveal my new shirt."

I clench my fists, sputtering, "Oh, really?"

"Yep!" She laughs obnoxiously while peeling off her sweatshirt.

My eyes widen with fury. Ferocity jolts through my veins as I read the writing on her shirt: I GOT UR MAN.

"I had it specially made," she boasts, batting her mascara-clad eyelashes. "Payback's a bitch, ain't it?"

I want to gnaw her tiny brain out with my teeth! I shout, "You little b—"

"Beautiful day today, isn't it?" Ms. Hoopensteiner interrupts us. "Let's get along, girls."

Still fuming, I try to swallow the hate phlegm that's clogging my throat as I turn my attention toward our elfish gym teacher.

"If you lovely girls can find the time around your busy feuding schedules"—Ms. Hoops smiles at us graciously—"I'd like to start class now."

I agree reluctantly. Then, I glance back at Britney with an I'll-get-you-later sneer. She points to the writing on her shirt and covers a devious smile with her other hand. My body feels like it's about to burst like a volcano. I feel like spewing molten red hot lava all over Britney and her man-stealing skintight T.

Ms. Hoops waddles to the net set up in the middle of the gymnasium and asks, "Can anyone tell me what sport we'll be playing today?"

Although the tennis ball rack and rackets on the side of the court make this answer perfectly obvious, no one offers a response.

"Well." The teacher laughs. "We've got a bunch of sleepy sulkers here today! We're playing tennis, girls. I'd let you play on the courts outside, but it's still too wet from this weekend's rain." She points to the rackets and says, "Let's all grab a racket."

I walk close on Britney's heels, trying to intimidate her. My tactics don't work. She groans in disgust. "You're such a lezza-saurus. Get off me!"

"Oops! I'm sorry!" I say, bumping into her as I pick up a racket. "You've gotten so fat there just isn't enough room not to bump into you."

She hisses, "Shut it, fugly Skunk Skank."

Ms. Hoops continues her tennis introduction. She explains the rules, her love of the sport, and finally ends her speech by requesting volunteers to demonstrate.

Britney jumps excitedly, raising her hand.

"Thank you, Miss Taylor!" the squatty gym teacher says with surprise. "C'mon up here!"

My stomach gurgles in disgust as Britney saunters to Ms. Hoops in her tight pink I GOT UR MAN T-shirt.

The teacher clasps her tiny hands together, bowing forward slightly as she speaks. "Have you ever played tennis before, Miss Taylor?"

"Since I was four," Britney responds, towering over the teacher in an arrogant stance.

"Perfect!" Ms. Hoops claps. "Now we need one more volunteer for a demo singles game."

She looks around at the group of girls.

Britney interjects politely, "If you don't mind, I'd love to ask April Bowers to play with me."

"Uh . . . I don't think that's such a good idea," the teacher disagrees.

Britney tilts her head innocently, opening her eyes wide like a harmless, sweet puppy. "But why? I really want to make amends. This can be a truce match. I'd like to put our problems behind us. You yourself have said that sports open the bridge to comradeship, right?"

I grimace at the gym teacher, noticing that she's buying into Britney's BS.

"Well, yes . . . I *did* say that! So glad you're willing to play nice!" She puts her arm around Brit. "To forgive one another is to love one another. And love, my friends"—she pauses to look at her students—"is what makes the world go round."

"You're so right, Ms. Hoops," Britney brown-noses. "I shouldn't have ever judged April for having foot fungus and herpes."

I grunt loudly, growing more and more furious by the second.

"Good, Britney! Tolerance is an important step on the journey to friendship." Ms. Hoops extends her hand to me. "Are you willing to accept Miss Taylor's request, Miss Bowers?"

Tempted to say no, since I've never played tennis in my life, I picture Britney's head as the tennis ball and can't help but agree to the death match.

"You bet!" I exclaim, dusting my pads off.

Ms. Hoops looks at me, puzzled. "You don't have to wear elbow pads and shin guards to play tennis."

I smile kindly at her, and then extend a fake smile to Britney.

"Oh, yes, I do," I say sharply. Battles call for body armor.

"Well then," she says, "go ahead and start your tennis demo, girls."

Seventeen minutes later, I wake up in the nurse's office with a cool, damp cloth over my eye and a massive headache.

"W-wh-what happened?" I moan, trying to prop myself up on the stiff cot. I notice my shin guards and red gym shorts, and suddenly realize that my attempt to kill Britney Taylor with a tennis ball probably didn't go as planned.

The nurse rushes to my side. "Oh! No, no! Honey, don't strain yourself!"

I plop my head back down in misery on the paper-thin pillow.

"Don't be alarmed, but I think you might have a black eye," she says, adjusting her white apron. Her sharp features reflect the light of the adjacent window.

"Why?" I mumble softly like I'm in a death scene of a movie.

"Well, dear, Ms. Hoopensteiner said you took a pretty hard hit." She walks to her medical supply station. "Two of them, actually."

She bends down to open the small stainless steel refrigerator and grabs an ice pack. She walks back and hands it to me. "Here you go; try an ice pack."

"My chin hurts, too," I complain, trying to move my bottom jaw from side to side.

"I believe that was the hit that knocked you out, dear. The first ball hit you in the eye."

"And I kept playing? After being hit in the eye with a speeding tennis ball?" I mutter, utterly confused. "Could I even see?"

"Not sure." The nurse puzzles over this for a moment and

continues, "But Ms. Hoopensteiner said you were a real trouper out there. You refused to take a time-out."

Sitting at her desk, looking into a small round mirror propped in the corner, she tucks a bobby pin into her tightly wound bun to straighten it. "Anyway, rest up for now. Your mom is on her way to pick you up."

chapter eighteen

Although my eye is as swelled as a large blowfish, I'm feeling a little better by dinnertime. My mom has been treating me like a baby all day, even after Dr. Oarman assured her that I wasn't going to go blind or die. I just have a bit of a concussion . . . but this isn't as concerning as the fact that I can't look into a mirror without terrifying myself.

My brother is getting a charge out of my new look. He snickers at the dinner table. "Can someone please pass me the black eye?"

I try to glare at him with my usual dirty look, but my eye feels like it may pop out of its socket. It's so much harder to give successful dirty looks with only one working eye.

"Aaden!" my mom snaps. "Don't make light of April's injury! I didn't raise you that way!"

"Sorry, Ma." He laughs. "I meant to say . . . would you please pass the eye patch—er, I mean potatoes?"

She stares at him with her dangerously famous don't-try-me-again look as she passes him the mashed potatoes.

My dad inspects me from across the table. "Yep, Bean, you've got a shiner there."

"Don't remind me."

After dinner, I sulk upstairs, hunkering down on my bed. Since my face feels as though a bomb goes off on it every time I move my head, I try to stabilize it among some pillows.

"Don't get too comfortable! You heard Dr. Oarman. You're not supposed to fall asleep with a concussion! Don't lie down on your bed," my mom yells from the kitchen amid running dishwater and clanking pans.

"I know!" I respond firmly, while secretly refusing to get up from my comfortable position.

Annoyed at my current Cyclops condition and the fact that I can't fall into a deep, deep sleep to forget it all, I decide to call Haley. I tell her all the heinous details of the day—the T-shirt, the tennis massacre . . . and all about the blue and purple hideousness bubbling rapidly from my face. I also explain that I didn't technically break my promise to her or the Oath—I would have asked Matt if he wasn't already taken by the I-GOT-UR-MAN-T-shirt-wearing tramp.

"You know what you have to do now, don't you?" Haley says after a brief solemn silence.

"Lock myself in my closet for forty-seven and a half years?" I say, knowing this is precisely the amount of time I need to recover from the trauma of today's events.

"No, April, c'mon! You need to fulfill the Lawbreaker Oath more than ever now! Britney has it coming to her. You better be willing to dish it out."

"Maybe when my face deflates," I say. "But for now I have to worry about finding a date to the spring formal. No one's going to want to be seen with Sloth from *The Goonies*."

Haley laughs, then quickly tries to comfort me. "I doubt you look like Sloth, April."

The truth is that I look like a complete circus freak. This is exactly what Britney wanted. She took my hot guy, and she stole my looks . . . leaving me with no formal date and a speed bump on my face.

Going to school looking like an inflamed mutant the day after being attacked by a small yellow ball is truly distressing. I ignore Matt in homeroom, which isn't hard, because my left eye is swollen to Jupiter, and he sits to my left. I can feel him staring at me, probably dying to know what happened, but I choose to snub him anyhow. I'm still enraged over the whole Britney Taylor I GOT UR MAN thing. Not to mention, I told him that I already have a date to the formal, and I don't want him questioning me any more about my plans.

Mr. Stuart jumps in horror when he sees me. "Holy smokes, April! What happened?"

"Tennis balls are hazardous weapons," I respond coolly.

The class laughs. I'm happy that others find humor in my suffering.

By lunchtime, I feel like I'm about to go postal from having to explain what happened to me 639 times. There are so many different rumors about the tennis massacre circulating around school; everyone is overly eager to hear the real story from the one-eyed horse's mouth. I'm relieved to finally get a chance to sit with my friends in the cafeteria . . . the ones who understand and support my trials and tribulations.

"Jeez, it looks worse than it did this morning." Ashley gawks.

I begin to rethink the whole supporting trials and tribulations thought I had a minute ago. "Thanks, Ash."

"Oh, no . . . I didn't mean it like that. I mean, it doesn't look that bad . . . just worse than before . . . Er, you know what I mean. Does it still hurt?"

"No, actually, it's similar to getting a massage," I reply in a monotone.

Rachel laughs, slipping a straw into her soda. "Not the brightest question, Ashley."

"I still don't know how you managed to refrain from strangling her when she showed you that shirt." Mel shakes her head, spreading cream cheese on a sesame bagel.

"Oh, believe me, I wanted to."

"What stopped you?"

"I wanted to spare Ms. Hoops the violence. The Cookie Monster from *Sesame Street* is probably violent in her eyes," I explain, tapping my eye to see if it still hurts. Yes, it does.

"She should be suspended. Her eighty-miles-per-hour tennis serve should be considered a deadly weapon! She could've killed you!" Mel says dramatically.

I shudder at the thought of police filing into the gymnasium crime scene to draw a chalk line around my lifeless tennis-ball-beaten body. How was I supposed to know that Britney is some tennis champ with a wicked fast serve? Maybe I am lucky to have come out of this ordeal alive . . . as a Cyclops.

Ashley pops a Dorito in her mouth and changes the subject. "I just hope the whole Britney-Matt thing isn't going to deter you from going to the spring formal."

"Oh, that little thing? Why would it?" I grind my teeth, still jealous.

"Really, April, you have to go," Mel says.

The girls look at me wide-eyed, nodding in agreement. Do they not see the hideous bruise mound that's formed on my face? How do they expect me to get a date looking like this? And it's not like I can go alone. Matt will think I got ditched—and that will no doubt make me look like a ginormous loser.

"How am I going to find anyone willing to go with me while I look like this?"

The girls glance at my eye, wincing sympathetically.

Rachel tries to cheer me up, pointing to a cute sophomore at the table next to us. "Look, Jerry Henderson is checking you out right now. I'm sure he'd love to go with you . . ."

Aggravated, I groan, "He's not checking me out! He's staring like the rest of the cafeteria at the purple mountain growing out of my face! I'll probably end up going with a complete loser, like . . . like . . . Delvin McGerk!"

Expressions of hopeful optimism dance on their faces. I can tell what they're thinking, and it makes me nauseous.

"Nope! No way! Not a chance! Don't even think about it! King Stalker McGerk is not an option!" I burst out emphatically.

"Well, at least you know he won't say no," Ashley reasons.

Crossing my arms in defiance, I repeat, "Not an option!"

"He's not that bad. You might be able to mold him into a hottie," Rachel says brightly.

"Nope. Not happening," I retort, becoming more nauseated by the second. "I'd rather not go to the formal at all . . . and be called out for lying about having a date."

Melanie directs her bagel at me assertively. "Don't even say that, April! You're going! You have to go! You can't let Britney get away with that!" She redirects her bagel at my swollen eye. "You know she wants to screw up your formal. Actually, she wants to screw up your *life!* Obviously fake Troy wasn't enough. We need to put our Lipstick Lawbreaker Law back into action."

This reminds me of my conversation with Haley last night. Lee was very adamant about me enforcing Lipstick Lawbreaker sabotage on Britney at the spring formal. Melanie notices that I'm absorbing her counsel. This adds more fuel to her fire.

She continues, "Delvin McGerk isn't even technically a loser. Not enough people know him for him to be classified as a loser."

"Mel, his nickname's King Stalker McGerk of *Loserhood* for a reason," I say matter-of-factly.

Melanie gets annoyed. "Seriously, April! Stop being so superficial! Isn't that what irks you so much about Britney? My point is, you shouldn't care who you take as long as you go!"

"Yeah, I mean, look at Mel." Ashley giggles. "She's going with a cross-dresser."

Mel lifts her chin rebelliously. "What's wrong with that? He has a great shoe collection."

"Too bad they're all size thirteen," Rachel reminds her.

"Regardless, my spring formal date proves my point. It doesn't matter who you go with. Not to mention," Melanie says, "I'm planning on hanging out with you guys the whole time anyhow. Like I said, dates don't matter."

Ashley's eyes narrow slyly. "Our top priority shouldn't be our dates . . . It should be making Britney's night miserable!"

The girls all agree vehemently. They begin to brainstorm sabotage ideas. I tune them out once they mention the movie *Carrie* and something about pig's blood.

Jessica stares at me in Spanish class. Even though we haven't talked since she confronted me about the fake Troy Hoffman incident, I have a feeling she's going to try to talk to me today. My face has been a curiosity sparker all day, and knowing Jessica, she's probably dying to say her two cents about it.

Predictably, she taps me on the shoulder as we're leaving class.

"Sorry about your eye, April," she says, biting her shiny, glossed bottom lip.

"At least I have a second one," I say.

She laughs, soon realizing that I'm not joking. "Oh. Right. Well, I'm supposed to give you a message from Brit."

Just her name sends a shock wave of loathing through my bones. I quiver with hatred and say, "Are you Brit-brat's personal Lipstick slave now?"

Jessica rolls her eyes, flipping her long dark hair back. "Look, I'm just relaying a message for a friend."

"A friend would let you wear the formal dress you want," I respond, referring to the rumor floating around school that Britney has banned her Lipstick Law followers from buying formal dresses nicer than hers. In fact, I heard that she and Jessica had a bit of a falling-out this past weekend over it. Obviously, since Jess is doing Brit's dirty work today, they must have mended things.

Jessica raises an eyebrow suspiciously. "How do you know about that?" She shakes her head and changes the subject, not giving me time to tell her that the whole school knows it. "Anyway, about her message—"

"Isn't my black eye message enough?"

"Yeah, well . . . she just wants to let you know that if you hadn't broken the Lipstick Laws, none of this would have happened." She points to my face and scrunches her nose.

I laugh mockingly. "That's her message?"

"Yes." She looks confused.

I purse my lips, straighten my back, and stand tall before speaking. "Do me a favor and thank Britney for her ludicrous Lipstick Laws . . . and let her know that I'm happy I broke them."

Jess's dark eyes widen. "You're *happy* you broke them? But *why?*"

"Heck yeah, I'm happy!" I say. "I wouldn't have met my three good friends otherwise."

She smiles briefly. "I'll give her the message." Then, she inches closer. "But . . . what about Matt Brentwood? You don't care that Britney's going to the spring formal with him?"

I try to hide my envy. "Gosh no, Jess! We're just friends. Besides, someone else asked me a long time ago." I glance at her to see if she believes my outlandish fib. I'm satisfied with her puzzled expression and say, "Well, see ya . . . I've gotta get to class."

I walk away and slip into the girls' bathroom before she has time to ask me any more questions. My blood is boiling in the stall. Groaning with anxiety, I grasp that I've just lied for the second time about having a date. And by doing so, I've made my spring formal date quest even more urgent than it already was. I take a few deep breaths to help calm my nerves.

"Just make it through the day, April," I coach myself quietly.

I smooth my curls down and check on my Kleenex cleavage. My humongous eye socket blocks the view out of my left eye. Shutting it tightly, I twinge in pain. I peer down my shirt with my right eye and tuck some escaping tissues back into my boob-icle cubicle bra cups before heading to class. I dart down the half-empty hallway, knowing I'm bound to be late.

During seventh-period science, while the teacher is giving a passionate lecture on the myths and facts of global warming, I can only think about two things: Mr. Hottie-Body Brentwood going to the formal with Britney . . . and me going to the formal alone. I bubble with spite in my seat. How can he like her? Can he not see that she's the Antichrist? And why did I lie about having a date? I could have just said I'm going on vacation that weekend . . . or I have a wedding to go to . . . or my brother is having a lobotomy. But no, I set myself up to be the laughingstock of the Lipstick Lawlords. What's worse is, I look like a beat-up, one-eyed circus freak now. My chances of finding a date willing to take a Cyclops to the formal are zilch at this point.

Well, on second thought . . . as discussed in lunch, there's one person who won't mind going to the formal with a Cyclops, and he approaches me as usual after class.

"Hi, April Bow—"

I cut him off impatiently. "April! Just April, Delvin! No need for last names here!"

He tries to shove his hands in his pant pockets, quickly realizing that his jeans are way too tight to fit a quarter into, let alone a pair of geek hands. He decides instead to fidget with the straps of his huge backpack and says, "That looks like it hurts."

"What, this?" I ask, pointing to the purple speed bump on my face. "Just a little."

I try to hustle down the hallway. Unfortunately, his legs are longer than mine, and he has no problem keeping up with me.

"Got my license last week. My dad's buying me a new Camaro before the spring formal." He glances at me awkwardly out of the corner of his eye, hoping to get my attention.

Half listening, I glance back at him. "Congrats, McGerk, that's cool."

Smiling pitifully, he blurts, "Perfect ride for the formal, don't ya think?"

"Sure," I say, unimpressed.

I stop at the water fountain, hoping he'll keep going past. He doesn't. I grab my thick hair to the side and bend down to take a sip of water.

Delvin leans on the wall with his bony elbow and continues, "So, I was gonna ask you . . ."

I choke on the cold stream of water, splattering it onto my cheeks. I know what's coming. I stand up, cornered between him and the water fountain. Wiping the excess water from my face, I wait in dread for him to continue talking.

"What d'ya say we go together?"

I stare at him, expressionless.

"To the spring formal," he adds with a cheesy wink.

Even after my friends insisted he's not that bad and that he's a perfectly moldable date, my immediate response is no, of course. However, as I'm pondering how I should decline civilly, I catch a glimpse of Britney Taylor hanging on Matt Brentwood at his locker.

"Bitch," I mutter quietly.

Delvin's shoulders slump and his smile fades. "Excuse me?"

Many thoughts speed through my mind at once:

- Matt and Britney dancing closely at the prom.
- The Lipstick Lawlords heckling me mercilessly about not having a date.
- Getting rejected by potential dates because of my current Cyclops condition.
- The beautiful dress Haley gave me collecting dust in my closet.

And . . .

- Melanie calling me superficial.

Finally, I picture Delvin's semi-hot photo on the Christmas card and think to myself: minus his hair and wardrobe, maybe he's not nerd-boy of the universe. Would it be possible to mold him into a decent formal date?

Grudgingly, I realize that under my current circumstances, he may be the only date I'll find. I peer over angrily at Matt and Brit's flirt festival before looking Delvin in his pleading gray eyes and agreeing bitterly, "Sure, Delvin."

My body floods with regretful repulsion immediately after uttering those two simple words.

It's obvious from Delvin's submissive sulking that he's prepared himself for a denial. He bows his head and puts his hand up to dismiss looming pity, regurgitating his rehearsed rejection speech: "No, I understand. It's okay . . . It would have been fun . . . but really, I understand. Wait." It takes him a few seconds to process my response. He looks at me in disbelief. "What? Y-You'll go with me?"

I wobble with nausea.

"Under two conditions!" I point at him seriously. "Never say my first and last name together again . . . and let me give you a makeover."

"Makeover?" he repeats apprehensively. "But I got rid of my braces and glasses. What else is there to do?"

"Oh, Delvin, Delvin, Delvin . . ." I slowly point from his tight jeans to his snugly tucked plaid shirt to his horribly parted floppy mop top and sigh fretfully. "There's lots more to do!"

He pauses, genuinely considering my contingencies. Then he looks me in my nonbulging eye and squirms in delight. "Okay . . . It's . . . it's a deal, April Bow— Um, I mean, April! I'm yours—mold me like Play-Doh!"

He extends his right hand for a let's-seal-the-deal handshake.

Trying to control my gag reflex, I say firmly, "Let's just skip the handshake."

It doesn't take long before I realize the huge mistake I've made. Delvin McGerk is my spring formal date. My life is officially over.

chapter nineteen

After committing social suicide by agreeing to go to the spring formal with King Stalker McGerk of Loserhood, I know that much work has to be put into his makeover to ensure that I don't die in a humiliation hurricane. My first step, of course, is to raid Delvin's closet to see if there's anything salvageable in the wreckage. My second step for today is schooling him on acceptable versus unacceptable social skills. If he wants me to go to the formal with him, he needs to look and act normal at school, too!

Mrs. McGerk greets me at the front door. She curiously glances at the cover-up makeup caked on my black eye before bursting, "Come in, April!" She chokes me into submission with her overwhelming perfume and strangling hug. "I just always knew you and Delvin would make the cutest couple!"

"Oh yeah?" I mutter absently, standing motionless in her death grip, smothered against her plump bosom like a bug smashed on a windshield.

"Your mother and I had so much fun in college," she whispers, leaning down. "Probably too much fun . . . but we won't tell the misters that."

She walks through the front hallway, motioning for me to follow her. It's like a museum of the evolution of Delvin. His pictures are plastered on every inch of the foyer walls. I stop to inspect a grade school picture of him. Apparently, this is when he became a permanent resident of Loserhood. The poor boy didn't have a chance sporting an oversize polka-dotted bow tie and those green suspenders . . . not to mention the same floppy, parted brown hair he's still famous for.

Mrs. McGerk pauses briefly to admire another framed memory. "He's just grown up so quickly!" she gushes, lovingly stroking a horrendous picture of a young Delvin in front of the Magic Kingdom at Disney World. Her eyes gloss with nostalgia. While she's reminiscing, I pray that the bright orange fanny pack he was wearing in this picture has since been donated.

Delvin's mom pats down her overprocessed blond hair like she's stuffing her wistful remembrances back into her head, and smiles.

"I'm sure that you guys will have so much fun together." She nudges me. "Not too much fun, though, if you know what I mean . . ."

Eww! The thought of whatever she's hinting at nearly makes me lose the caesar salad I ate for lunch. She leads me into their kitchen, where I take a seat on a tall stool at the large kitchen island. Mrs. McGerk saunters to the refrigerator in her tight pants. I guess Delvin isn't the only one with an affinity for Saran Wrap trousers.

She opens the fridge and asks, "Can I get you something to drink, honey?"

"No, thanks," I respond with a polite smile. Mrs. McGerk seems like a nice hostess, but clearly, I'm here to work, not visit over drinks.

Soon after, Delvin enters the kitchen, looking awestruck by my presence. He smiles awkwardly at me.

"Mom," he says, "why are you trying to kidnap my date?"

They laugh, looking at me to share in their amusement. I choke out a chuckle . . . which is more like a gurgle that's bubbled up nauseatingly from my stomach at the thought of Delvin calling me his date.

"We were just having some girl talk, Deli. I'll let you two have some time alone now." She winks at me.

Walking into Delvin's room is like a time warp. I feel as though I'm being sucked into his boyhood bedroom by a large, musty vacuum. The baby blue walls and big stenciled airplanes covering the room make me woozy. Other than his mother, I have no doubt that I'm the only girl who's ever entered his juvenile pilot palace.

He points to the walls. "I used to like airplanes. Still do, actually."

"You don't say, Deli," I tease.

"You caught my nickname."

"Yeah. I'd like to order a pastrami sandwich, please."

He stares at me curiously for a second, until he realizes that I'm joking. Then he snorts like an out-of-shape ape trying to run on a treadmill. This indigestible snort is the catalyst that makes me delay the closet raid and head right to my lesson on social skills.

"I made this for you," I say sharply, pulling out a chart from my large tote. "It summarizes how you should act"—I pause, handing it to him sternly—"and how you shouldn't."

Delvin's face becomes red as he studies it.

"No science talk?" he mutters.

"None! Leave that for class."

He continues to read, shaking his head, "No snorting? I don't snort!" He laughs, ending it with a snort.

"Clearly"—I point to him—"you just did."

Reading more of my long list, he argues nervously, "I-I can't help it if I stutter when I'm excited."

I cringe and plead, "Well, maybe you can try."

He reads more and inquires, "You don't want me to let you know when our mothers talk?"

"Delvin, they're friends! Friends talk! This isn't news!" I explain impatiently.

Then his shoulders slump as he reviews the "Do" portion of the chart.

"I don't know anything about sports; how am I supposed to hold an educated conversation about football?"

I say to clarify, "It doesn't have to be educated. Just show an interest in it."

He finishes reading my lengthy list and looks up at me gloomily. "You don't like anything about me. Do you?"

"Well." I'm caught off-guard and begin to feel bad. "That's not true."

Delvin shakes his head, pointing at my social chart. "That's not what this tells me."

"Delvin, it's just a simple guideline," I reason with him. "You told me you're up for a makeover. Are you going to back out on our deal?"

"I-I . . . just didn't think you meant a personality makeover, too."

"I'm not trying to change you . . . just enhance you," I lie through my teeth.

He doesn't respond.

"You're a formal date in training right now. This is just part of your orientation," I say brightly, thinking this line sounds strangely familiar.

He looks down, still unresponsive.

"It's nothing against you. Don't take it personally." I smile.

Halfheartedly, he mumbles, "I guess."

I start to feel guilty. Even though Delvin's annoying, I'd never want to purposefully hurt his feelings. Maybe I am being a bit harsh. I mean, I listed every annoying thing he does (which happens to be twenty-five tremendously irritating Delvin quirks) in the "Don't" area of the chart . . . and I listed all of their opposite actions in the "Do" area. That is a bit of a personal blow, I guess. But . . . this is in his best interest, right? Of course it is! I'm not trying to be mean. I'm doing what's best for him. I shouldn't feel bad. I'm helping him out! Some people pay for this kind of a service! He's lucky! He's a big boy and needs to be able to handle constructive criticism!

"Stop pouting, Delvin; I'm not trying to hurt your feelings. I'm just trying to *help* you. But if you don't want my help—"

"No . . . I do!" he says desperately. He scans the social chart again and smiles sheepishly. "It's okay. You're right. I'll try to work on it all."

"There's no harm in trying, right?" I say, feeling a combination of relief and guilt. "Okay, now, on to your closet . . ."

The next day, we go to the mall for a brand-new wardrobe. Unsurprisingly, there was nothing much to save in Delvin's closet. I couldn't very well leave him to create outfits from the sparse couple of T-shirts, one pair of gym pants, swim trunks, and the few pairs of socks that I'm allowing him to keep.

"It's always best to start with a clean slate," I assure him, piling more and more try-on choices onto his outstretched arms.

"Sure," he mumbles through the trendy apparel stacked up to his head.

"I think it's time to try it all on." I guide him to an open dressing room.

I'm anxious to see Delvin's first outfit. I grow concerned after many minutes go by and several thumps, bumps, and a few clunks come from behind his door.

"You okay in there?"

"Fine!" he squeaks.

Eventually he emerges, looking like he's just changed in front of a giant windmill. His face is flushed, and his floppy hair is disheveled . . . but the new jeans and polo shirt look great!

"I love it, McGerk!" I jump excitedly as he approaches the three-way mirror to look for himself.

He pulls the sides of the jeans out by the pockets and shakes them to show their roominess. "Aren't these too baggy?"

"Jeans aren't supposed to fit you like tights! They're perfect," I say forcefully. "This outfit's a keeper! Next outfit, please . . ."

Delvin continues to appraise each new look skeptically in the three-way mirror. Luckily, he's easy to convince, and we leave store after store with a steadily growing wardrobe in tow.

"I promise you, McGerk, you're gonna love your new look."

He glances at me, struggling with his overflowing bags. "As long as you do."

Next, we make our way to a tux shop to pick out his spring formal duds. He immediately migrates to a hideous royal blue zoot suit with a matching cane.

My mouth drops in horror. "Are you kidding?"

He looks at me with a kid-in-a-candy-store grin, and I soon realize he isn't.

"Oh, no, no, no!" I scold, pulling him far away from the atrocity. I redirect him to a conservative, stylish black tuxedo that I can't help but picture Mr. Hottie-Body Brentwood looking delicious in.

"You can never go wrong with classic black," I explain.

"Once you go black, you never go back . . . or so I've heard." He snorts like a swine, quickly slapping his hand over his mouth. "Sorry. Didn't mean to snort."

"It's okay. You're trying." I humor him, handing over the tux.

"Black is supposed to be slimming, right?" He holds it up to his thin frame.

"Yeah, but you don't need any help in that department."

He tries the tuxedo on, and I'm actually pleased with it. Excluding his deplorable hair and hampering social skills, he could potentially trick an overgrown nutterputz into thinking he's a decent catch.

Holding his arms up awkwardly, he asks, "Does it pass the test?"

"Hmm." I smile, admiring the crisply pressed tux approvingly. "Looking good, Delvin . . . but let's do something different with your mop top."

"Mop top?"

"Yeah—your hair. Judging from the pictures plastered all over your front hall, you've had the same cut since first grade."

He pats his floppy dark mop and says, "Yeah . . . so? What's wrong with it?"

"Ummm . . . you're in high school now." I state the obvious. "You need a new 'do."

Reluctantly, he agrees. "Call me Play-Doh."

I drop him off at a hair salon in the mall, leaving his vulnerable out-of-date hair in the hands of a hairdresser named Jade. Her skunk-patched hair threw me off at first, but she promised she could give him a modern, stylish "Abercrombie model" haircut that I'll love. I pray that she sticks to the plan and he doesn't come out with a rainbow mohawk. On the other hand, even that would be an improvement at this point.

chapter twenty

Finally having some time to myself, I browse the mall on my own behalf. I decide to use the free time to look for a new bra, since none of my bras work with the low V front and crisscross back of my formal dress. Not to mention, even though I'm a tissue-stuffing savant, I need to find something more natural to help me in the woman-sprout department for the spring formal. Haley told me about these amazing boobicle cubicle chestoid enhancers at Victoria's Secret that look like raw chicken cutlets. They're flesh colored and they even jiggle—oh, what I wouldn't give to have some bona fide jiggle!

On my way to the lingerie store, sale signs in the glass windows of Express scream my name. I'm pulled to the store like a magnet to a fridge, and I begin to peruse the sale racks. Before long, I regret my store detour when I hear a familiar voice.

"Erin, you are *so* not a size four. Stop trying to pretend like you are!"

Oh my gosh, it's Britney Taylor and the Lipstick Lawlords looking at jeans near the front of the store. How could I be so shortsighted to venture into Express on a Sunday? This store is their place of worship on the holy day.

What should I do? Where should I go? There's no way I can leave without them seeing me. They're between me and the exit. Ducking behind a circular floor rack, I pray they don't come any closer.

"Have you dropped something?" a fellow shopper asks curiously.

"No . . . no . . . ummm . . . just tying my shoes," I say quietly, trying not to be heard by the encroaching Lawlords.

Peering down at me suspiciously, the lady notices my shoelace-less shoes; she huffs and mutters something snarky about teenagers before moving on to the next rack of clothes.

The Lawlords' voices grow louder. I can tell they're approaching steadily.

"Stay away from the sale racks, Jess; you know it's always last season's trash," I hear Brianna lecturing.

I just don't understand Bri's phobia of sales. I'm sure it's just another way for her to brag about money. Her family is richer than double chocolate fudge, and she uses every opportunity she can to display that. Mel and I are positive that the only reason Britney is friends with her is for her generous holiday and birthday gifts.

I gulp with worry as the circular clothing rack begins to spin in front of me.

"Yeah, but this stuff is fifty percent off," Jessica points out on the opposite side of my hiding spot. "Last season or not, that's a good deal!"

God, help me. If they see me, I'll never hear the end of it. How will I explain hiding like a moron behind a rack of clothes? And no way, no how am I going to pop up like a jack-in-the-box to face them. I have to find a better hiding place, but they're way too close for me to crawl inconspicuously to another spot.

"Shut up!" Brit says. "Fifty percent? That's like half off!"

I see the girls' feet joining Jess on the opposing side of my hiding spot. At this point, I feel I have no choice but to scurry inside the circular rack like a mouse burrowing into a hole. I tunnel my way through the hanging clothes, crouching quietly near the metal stand in the middle of the clothing carousel.

"This thing's sort of wobbly," Erin mentions, most likely noticing the force of my tunneling.

I hold my breath, hoping they don't investigate further . . . as this, out of all hiding scenarios, would be the hardest to explain. "Oh, don't you know? The best sales are always inside the rack." "Don't mind me; I'm just fixing the stand. I work here now." "Hiding? No, I'm not hiding! I'm simply trying to see if the colors look as vibrant in dim light." I try to think of ways to explain myself—all completely useless.

This has to be the lamest thing I've ever done in my life; well, second to signing the Lipstick Oath. Why couldn't I just walk past them with my head held high like they don't bother me? Why don't I feel confident when I'm outnumbered? Why does Britney still affect me like this? Why am I huddled between sale items?

Although I'm relieved that no one has inspected the seemingly unstable rack, my heart skips a beat when I hear my name brought up while they skim the clothes surrounding me like a shield.

"Did you see what April Bowers had on the other day? Can we say hideous-mart clearance rack vulture?" Britney laughs. "I bet she's already ravaged this sale here. I don't think she ever buys anything full price."

Double gulp—little do they know . . . Not only have I already examined the sale, I'm *inside* it!

"I still can't believe Matt was planning on asking that freak funnel."

My ears immediately perk up at the mention of Matt's name. Ask me? Ask me what?

"Yeah, how did you convince him not to?" Brianna says.

Leaning closer to their group, I strain to hear through the clothing.

"I told him that she already had a date and asked him to be my date before he could ask her about it. Really, it wasn't too hard to trick him. He's really dumb."

What? I gasp, quickly covering my mouth, but losing my balance at the same time. I catch myself from falling out of the rack, but overcompensate my save by banging my elbow on the metal stand.

"Ouch!" I yelp mindlessly, holding my funny bone, realizing I may have blown my cover.

"Did you hear something?"

"Yeah . . ."

"Sounded like . . ."

"That's weird . . ."

The girls circle the rack inquisitively. Their posh shined shoes cast a glare in my eyes. I'm tempted to attack Britney's Achilles' heel like a vicious rabid raccoon.

After a short guarded silence, I'm relieved when Jessica chimes in. "But Brit, you don't even like Matt, do you?"

"No . . . but it makes me happy to see that frizzy-haired freak funnel suffer."

Frizzy-haired? I am in silent torment over my curls as Jessica responds.

"Don't you think maybe it's time to move on?"

Did she just say what I think she did? Is she sticking up for me?

Right away, I can tell Britney is fuming over Jessica's comment. She stamps her foot heatedly. "Move on? You know some dipshits still harass me about the Troy thing, right? And the football team still doesn't talk to me . . . and Jamie Bradshaw made an anti-Brit-brat cheer about me . . . and it took me eight straight weeks of pathetic ass-kissing to get half of my popularity back . . . Not to mention, my first two formal choices rejected me . . . and you're telling me to lay off the person who's behind it all? Are you *crazy*?"

I see Erin's orange-stained ankles and Brianna's Jimmy Choo shoes step away from Jess to be closer to Britney. Obviously they're choosing sides.

"It's just . . . you've done a lot to her, too. Aren't you guys even?" Jessica's voice quivers.

"We'll be even when I run her out of the school. She's gotten everything she deserves, and there's plenty more to go around at the formal. She's not gonna know what hit her."

Triple gulp! I can hardly hold my composure as thoughts of Britney's spring formal revenge flood my mind.

Jessica takes a step back and says, "Can't we just try to have a good time instead? Isn't all this catfighting a little ridiculous?"

I faintly hear Erin and Bri whisper to each other. I'm sure they're reveling in the drama that's unfolding.

After a few seconds of what I'm assuming was a Britney Taylor death stare, she blurts, "Jessica, you're walking on thin ice! You better shut it, 'cause you're two steps away from being a social misfit like the rest of them. Remember Lipstick Law Seven—decisions are based on the group as a whole. Everyone who believes the best decision for the group is to make April's life hell, raise your hands."

I'm assuming Brianna, Erin, and Britney raise their hands. However, I still only have a clear view of their feet.

"We win," Britney taunts. She then storms out of the store with Brianna and Erin tagging along behind her. Jessica paces in the center aisle before eventually walking out to catch up with the other girls.

It's safe to come out from the rack now, but I'm trembling with anger and I can't manage to pick myself up. Matt was going to ask me to the spring formal! How dare she steal what's rightfully mine! How dare she try to ruin my formal! Who does she think she is? If anyone's not going to know what hit her, it's her . . . and I'll make sure of it!

After several minutes of private seething, I crawl out from the middle of the clothing carousel like a swamp creature. Several shoppers jump in surprise. I don't stick around long enough to explain myself.

Before returning to the hair salon to meet up with Delvin, I have a successful jaunt at Victoria's Secret. I buy an amazing plunging racerback bra and the chicken cutlet chestoid enhancers Haley told me about, but I can hardly be as excited about my purchase as I should be, because Britney Taylor's evil face is polluting my mind.

Like a Lipstick-Law-hating zombie, I make my way back to the salon and take a seat in the waiting area a few chairs away from Delvin without even realizing.

"April!" he says.

I jump, recognizing his voice, but not recognizing him. His hair is the perfect blend of scruffy ruggedness and pretty-boy styling. I can barely believe my eyes. I'm thoroughly impressed with Jade's hairdressing skills and hope that he tipped her well.

"Delvin?" I gawk at the made-over half-hottie sitting a few seats down, noticing that he also had time to change into one of his new outfits while waiting on me.

"Yeah, it's me." He smiles.

"Whoa! What a change! She even gave you some highlights," I say, amazed at the transformation. I smile, noticing a few giddy girls checking him out. "You're a stud now, McGerk. Do you like it?"

He blushes. "You were right. It makes a big difference. Anyway, where've you been?"

Delvin's new look had temporarily distracted me from thinking about everything that just went down with Britney. I shouldn't take away from his miraculous makeover moment, but remembering my mission, I refocus and say, "I don't want to get into it. Let's get out of here. I have a lot to do."

As soon as I get home, I immediately try to assemble an emergency Lipstick Lawbreaker meeting. Unfortunately, Ashley and Rachel are out with their Fairfield formal dates, but Melanie comes over immediately. I tell her the whole story, pacing around my room furiously. Melanie sits atop my bed with her mouth dropped wide open in shock.

She takes Britney's threats very seriously and says, "We have to do something to her before she does something worse to you!"

I nod. "I know! But what? It's not like we have a whole lot of time before the spring formal to think up an intricate plan."

"It doesn't have to be intricate. It just has to be effective."

We throw pathetic ideas back and forth for several minutes before I say, "It's too bad we can't just shove peanuts down her throat. She's allergic, you know."

Melanie looks as if a light bulb's gone off in her head. "That's brilliant!"

"Gosh, Mel, I can't stand her, but I don't wanna kill her!" I say.

"No, no . . . it won't kill her. It won't even hurt her. Her allergy isn't that bad. It's not serious, it's just cosmetic," Mel insists.

"How do you know?"

"Last year, when she was sleeping over at my house one night, she started pining over one of her trillion exes. She ended up cramming a jumbo pack of Reese's Peanut Butter Cups down her throat, saying that the hives aren't as bad as a broken heart. She got giant welts all over her body and her lips swelled up like the Goodyear Blimp, but she said she didn't care 'cause it was just the two of us."

"Really?" I say excitedly.

"Yeah, I started panicking because she seriously looked like a mutant hive-monger . . . but she calmed me down by saying that although it looks gross, it's not a serious allergy and the hives would go away in an hour."

"You're *sure* it's not serious?" I rehash.

"Positive! She admitted that sometimes, even though she's allergic, she can't say no to a peanut butter craving. If it were life threatening, she wouldn't go near the stuff!"

"Oh my gosh! How funny would it be to see her transform into a hived, hunky-lipped freak at the formal?" I say. "But there's no way she'd fall for eating peanut butter when she knows what's bound to happen to her."

"True." Melanie sighs; her chest deflates cheerlessly.

"Unless!" I jump excitedly, thinking of a genius idea. "We spike her drink with a little peanut oil!"

Melanie falls over on her side, laughing. She grabs a pillow, hugging it tightly to her stomach.

"I think we have a plan," she manages to say between giggles. "And while she's dealing with hideous hives, you can snatch Mr. Hottie-Body from her!"

I picture myself dancing the night away with Matt, and can't help but smile.

That night I have an incredible dream. I'm on a crowded dance floor looking drop-dead in my amazing dress. I zone in on Britney and Matt arguing in the middle of the crowd. I glide to the miserable couple and notice that Britney's holding a large pink mug to her side as she bickers. It's at this point that a bucket of peanut oil miraculously appears. I quickly pour it into her mug and wait for the magic to happen.

After one small sip, Britney begins to explode into a hive-monger mess. She tries to scream in horror, but she can't, as her lips have inflated to the point of malfunction. Her dress shoes swell and snap, revealing giant, bulging toes. The shiny pink sequins pop from her dress violently as she expands. The crowd runs for cover and the DJ abandons his post while Matt and I watch in awe as Britney erupts with huge hives, growing bigger and bigger by the second. Before long, she's so puffed up that she begins to float to the ceiling. Her engorged hands and fingers twitch frantically from the sides of her beach-ball body.

As she bounces in place between ceiling tiles and recessed lighting, Matt and I are left to ourselves to mingle flirtatiously.

"Wanna dance?" he says with a delicious smile.

"I thought you'd never ask," I say as he grasps me tightly to his body. I rest my head on his hard chest as we slow dance with Britney Taylor spinning above us like a gigantic hived disco ball.

chapter twenty-one

After an abundance of Britney Taylor peanut oil sabotage planning and last-minute McGerk editing, the day of the spring formal finally arrives. The last couple of weeks have been trying, since I can hardly glance at Matt without becoming a babbling moron. For some reason, knowing that he's Britney's pawn makes me even more nervous around him.

To get the courage I need to steal him away at the formal, I decide that I need a McGerk-esque makeover myself. The girls and I go to the same salon that gave him his miraculous hair makeover for our formal styles. With Britney's "frizzy-haired freak funnel" nickname engraved in my mind, I talk Jade into straightening my hair with an amazing CHI hair-straightening iron. Geniusly, she tucks the portion that Mel had to cut after Britney threw gum in my hair behind my ear with a fab-tastic barrette.

I barely recognize myself when I look in the mirror. My hair's so long and soft without it springing up into my dreaded curls. I love it and can't wait to see the new style paired with my gorgeous, flowing gown. If my hair doesn't make Matt melt, my dress surely will.

"Your hair looks amazing! It's so long and shiny!" the girls rave as we leave the salon.

"Thanks! You guys look amazing, too," I say, admiring Melanie's sleek up-do, Rachel's new layers, and Ashley's bold swept curls.

"You sure you don't want to come over this afternoon?" Melanie asks, hoping I'll change my mind.

"I'm sure. I don't need any blackmail pictures."

Much to my friends' and my parents' dismay, I'm standing firm on my decision not to attend Melanie's preformal picture party, which her parents are hosting at their house. As much as I thoroughly appreciate the time and effort Delvin has put into his makeover, I don't want photographic evidence of him being my date. If, by chance, I become famous in ten years' time, I don't want my date with King Stalker McGerk of Loserhood memorialized in a "Celebrities in High School" issue of a tabloid magazine.

As I'm putting on the finishing touches of my makeup, my mom enters my room.

"Thanks for knocking," I say flatly while smudging more cover-up on the faded bruise under my eye.

"My little girl looks grown," she gushes. "Stand up, honey! Let me see the dress!"

I humor her by standing up and whirling around . . . mainly because I can't pass up an opportunity to twirl in this dress. The light, silky fabric wisps around me as if I'm floating through the air, and my long, flowing hair dances elegantly with my dress.

"You look like a princess!" she says, glossy-eyed, taking a seat on my bed.

"Thanks, Mom. Too bad my date isn't Prince Charming."

"That's partly why I wanted to talk to you before he comes to pick you up." Her face becomes serious. "Please be nice to Delvin tonight. You know I'm friends with his mother . . . and he's a sweet boy. I don't want you to break his heart!"

I sigh and say, "Of course I'll be nice to him, but don't expect a romantic happily ever after."

"I'm not expecting anything other than friendship." She points at me. "And remember, friends are nice to each other, April."

Why is she lecturing me? Does she think I'm planning on taunting him? Please, I'm planning on hightailing it to the opposite side of the dance floor. I won't be around to be mean to him. Rolling my eyes, I agree with her. I don't bother arguing the fact that not everyone is nice to their friends. Britney Taylor is a prime example of that.

She scans me carefully. Her eyes stop at my chest, which is showcasing my new chicken cutlet boobicle cubicle chestoid enhancers. I gulp nervously, hoping she can't see any remnants of them poking out. I've been trying to conceal them, but depending on how I move, they may show a little bit out of the corners of my dress. Luckily, they blend in with my skin.

"You must be glad you didn't inherit my rinky-dink chest." She laughs, looking down at her flat upper body. "You must take after Dad's side."

I feel my face flush. Clearly, my mom has no idea that I'm an obsessed bosom sculptor and in fact, I've inherited her less-than-there chest. If she can't tell that I have bra enhancers under my dress, hopefully no one else will be able to, either.

I smile at her and say, "Must've got them from somewhere." Unfortunately, the somewhere I'm referring to happens to be Victoria's Secret, not Dad's side of the family.

My mom bounces to her feet; an airy smile creeps over her face. "Well, you look stunning. Let me at least take some pictures before Delvin picks you up."

I agree; after all, pictures of me are fine . . . pictures of me and Delvin are not.

Soon before my made-over date arrives, Haley calls to wish me luck.

"Good luck, Apes," she says. "Matt's not going to be able to resist you tonight. The hived peanut oil monster is gonna have nothin' on you!"

"Yep, cross your fingers for me. The trick will be to get it in her drink without her noticing," I say, inspecting the small vanilla extract bottle that I emptied and replaced with peanut oil.

"Just pray that Stalker McGerk leaves you alone long enough to get the job done," she warns.

Delvin's stalkerific tendencies have tortured my mind for the last week. That's why I plan on escaping his view as soon as we get to the formal convention center. Hopefully he doesn't secretly connect a GPS tracking device to my dress while I'm not looking.

Before I can reply, a horrendous noise comes from down the street. It seems to be getting closer and closer . . . sounding like a screaming cat on a broken-down carnival ride.

Screech . . . screech . . . hissssssssssss . . . clunk . . . clunk . . . pop-bang-pop!

"What's that?" I blurt loudly.

The phone slips from my hand as I run to the window to check out the ear-gnawing noise. To my horror, it's a beat-up turquoise Camaro with rust out the wazoo heading straight for my driveway. God help me; it's my spring formal date.

I should have known this was going to happen. Delvin isn't cool enough to have a nice ride. I was beginning to get suspicious when he still hadn't gotten his "new" car as of a few days ago. He had promised me that he'd have it in time for the formal. At this point, after seeing the beat-up gremlin parked in my driveway, I think I'd rather take a bus.

I hear the doorbell ring and my mom greeting Delvin, telling him how handsome he looks before calling up the stairs for me.

My gut stings as I slip the peanut oil bottle into my silver clutch. Checking the mirror one last time, I whisper to my reflection, "Why did you say yes? Good thing you're not a Lipstick Lawlord anymore. You'd be violating Lipstick Law Four."

As I reluctantly plod down the stairs to my made-over date, I can hardly believe my eyes. Is that Delvin McGerk? Yeah, I know he's been looking pretty good at school lately, and some girls have taken notice, but he hasn't been looking this good. If I didn't know that he's a tax-paying resident of Loserhood, I might even think he's hot. I smile briefly, realizing that the people at the formal may not recognize him, either. Unfortunately, this phenomenal moment is overshadowed by the junker car that's waiting for us in the driveway.

Delvin's jaw drops as I approach. His hands shake the plastic wrist corsage box that he's holding. "You look beautiful, April! Your hair is—"

"Straight!" I interject, running my hand through my sleek locks. It feels so good to do this without my fingers getting snarled by curls.

Nodding, he gapes and adds, "It looks fantastic!"

"Thanks, Delvin. You look really good, too. That thing, on the other hand . . ." I point out the window to his dilapidated Camaro.

My mom shoots me a stern look and says, "Time for the corsage and boutonniere!"

She rushes to the kitchen to get Delvin's boutonniere from the refrigerator. While Delvin places the rose and baby's breath corsage on my wrist, my brother and his friend Jeffrey Higgins appear from the game room . . . making themselves available for my humiliating exit.

My brother looks out the window at the hideous car. "Looks like you two love birds will be riding in style," he says.

My father quickly nudges him to shut up.

Jeffrey laughs like a goat. His Adam's apple trembles in amusement. What a disturbing moment to have sealed in my mind before the formal . . . almost as disturbing as my ride.

⁓⊙⁓

Being escorted to the spring formal in a train wreck hoopty is almost as humiliating as the tampon locker incident. I can hardly hear myself think over the clanging, grinding metal.

"You said you were getting a *new* Camaro!" I yell over the ruckus.

He can't hear me. "Huh?"

I repeat myself, even louder this time, "You said you were getting a NEW Camaro!"

"Well, it's not brand new . . . but it's new to me," he yells back.

"It was new in 1964, maybe!" I scream over the thunderous clanking and roaring muffler.

He corrects me, petting the dashboard with his right hand. "Actually, 1972. It's a gem."

"Keep both hands on the steering wheel!" I yell, afraid that this monster mess of metal is just one misstep away from disaster.

Once at the Rochester Convention Center, I direct Delvin to park as far away from the formal entrance as possible. I want to protect myself from being spotted getting out of this crusty, rusty, turquoise hunk of metal. Delvin lunges for his digital camera sitting in between the seats.

"No, no," I remind him. "Remember our deal: no pictures."

Mel is standing at the entrance waiting for me as promised. She's glancing impatiently at her cell phone, checking the time. Her face relaxes when she spots me. She grabs my arm and pulls me into the formal entrance hall. A NIGHT TO REMEMBER banners blow in the May night breeze as the door closes behind us.

"You look awesome! But . . . where've you been?" she questions.

"Delvin's car stalled eight times in my driveway before takeoff."

Melanie looks around through the crowd of dressed-up sophomores, right past Delvin. "Where's McGerk?"

He waves at her. She smiles back courteously, not realizing that it's him.

I laugh and point at Delvin. "In front of you."

Mel jumps. "No way! Shut up!"

Delvin puts his arms out as if he's presenting himself to the world for the first time. "It's me."

Gawking in astonishment, she blurts, "But . . . you look so . . . so . . . hot!"

"Ummm . . . thanks," he says, blushing.

I clear my throat loudly to interrupt her stare-fest. "I think we have something to attend to," I say.

"Right." She puts her attention back on me, grabbing my hand. "If you don't mind, Delvin, I'm gonna steal your date for a couple minutes."

Much to Delvin's disappointment, Mel pulls me into the large dance hall. Silver and blue streamers and balloons are overhead. I immediately spot a bubbling fountain of punch in the far corner of the room. It would be so much easier to just go ahead and spike the whole lot of punch, but I can't risk someone else having a serious peanut allergy and being rushed to the hospital because of my hostility toward Miss Dragon Wench Taylor. My job will be much harder having to slip it straight into her drink.

Examining the room, I lean in to Mel and say, "Where is she?"

She points to Britney. "How can you miss her? She's the only one wearing pink plastic wrap."

It feels as if I've been punched in the stomach as I zoom in to clear focus of Brit-brat in a skintight short pink dress with cleavage piling out the top of it. Matt's strong hand is wrapped around her waist as they're being swarmed by the Lipstick Lawlords. He looks absolutely delicious in his tux, but I'm afraid he's being contaminated by the head Lawlord.

"Look, she has a drink already!" Melanie points to the punch Britney's sipping. Her eyes light up as she glances down at my small handbag. "Do you have it with you?"

"Of course," I say, pulling out the little bottle, covering it with my grip. "I want to see the other girls first, though."

I always feel much more confident when I'm surrounded by people who support me. I know that with Melanie, Ashley, and

Rachel cheering me on, I'll have the courage I need to success-fully spike Britney's punch.

Tunneling through the crowd of formal attire, we meet up with the girls, their two dates, and Melanie's date, Mark Rhinehart. Surprisingly, he's looking extremely tall, masculine, and dapper in his tuxedo. The only thing slightly metrosexual about him is his meticulously styled blond hair. Ashley, Rachel, and I had wondered if he'd top his formal look off with high heels . . . or maybe go for the gold by wearing a dress. To Mela-nie's great relief, he's all male tonight, as far as I can see.

The girls flutter around me excitedly while their dates sub-merge into guy talk off to the side. We admire each other's dresses, makeup, hair, and shoes before getting down to business.

"You sure you're going to be able to pull it off?" Rachel asks, her hands fiddling nervously with the black satin straps of her dress.

"I think so," I say, trying to talk myself into it.

"Maybe we should get someone else to spike it," Ashley sug-gests, biting her lip with nerves.

"We can't trust anyone else to do it," Melanie responds loudly over the blaring DJ. "April can slip in behind her. Brit won't even see her."

Looking at the girls' anxious faces, I want to put their nerves to rest with a confident smile. Unfortunately, I'm not confident at all about this idea anymore. I don't know how I'm going to get near Britney without her noticing, let alone slip some pea-nut oil in her drink. This seemed like such a good idea in the planning stages, but now that I'm at the formal surrounded by a bunch of people, blaring music, and gaudy decorations, I'm suddenly rethinking our plan.

"You okay, April? D'ya want me to do it?" Rachel offers.

Forcefully, I say, "No . . . no . . . I'm fine. This is my job. I'm going to do it."

A rush of adrenaline comes over me. It's true—this is my job. Britney stole my guy. She gave me a black eye. She spread nasty rumors about me. She stuck tampons on my locker. And she cut a hole in my favorite jeans. It wouldn't make sense for anyone else to take revenge on her tonight but *me*.

chapter twenty-two

I'm on a mission. Intense with aim, I have zoned in on Britney's group as I inch my way closer and closer to them. My hand is so sweaty, I fear the peanut oil bottle may slip from it by accident. Gripping it tighter, I continue my mission march. I'm stopped briefly by several hair and dress compliments, but I don't let this distract me, as I have to get to Brat-ney before she gets to me.

I look back across the room at my friends, who excitedly showcase three thumbs-up signs, giving me a much-needed confidence boost. I'm within earshot now, and a twinge of longing surfaces as I'm close enough to hear Mr. Hottie-Body Brentwood's delicious laugh. Who in their group could possibly be making him laugh? They all have the sense of humor of a jammed doorknob.

I carefully dodge being spotted by slipping behind various sophomores while I wait for a clear opportunity to pour the mutant hive oil in her drink. I watch her closely as she brings her glass up to her lips, taking a small sip from it. Then she does what she's best at and gives a backhanded compliment to Erin.

"No, really, Erin, your dress looks great. It totally hides your stomach bulge."

My heart is pounding louder than the DJ's bass. Unscrewing the cap, I glide within arm's length of Britney's rearview, still making sure I'm out of eyeshot. This is it. She's holding her drink to the side of her, unprotected. I can just pour it right in there. As I bring the small bottle up in position to spike her drink, I shudder with fear when the group turns in my direction. Quickly, I stagger a few feet away to a snack table bordering the wall of the large dance hall, hoping they didn't see me. For a moment, I innocently look in every direction but theirs, until I get the nerve up to reevaluate the situation. Thankfully, I realize that Brianna was just pointing out the bathroom exit across the room, asking if anyone needs to go.

"Oh, thank goodness," I whisper, exhaling a heavy sigh of relief.

With their designer clutches in tow, the Lawlords part from their dates and strut to the ladies' room. I can barely believe my luck when the girls brush by me gossiping, without a second glance, placing their half-full punch glasses on the table just a few feet away.

Is this a joke? Can it be this easy? Watching to make sure that they are indeed going to the bathroom, I wait until they're no longer in sight. When the coast is clear, I sidestep nonchalantly to the unmanned drinks. Hovering over Britney's lipstick-stained punch glass, I fiddle nervously with the peanut oil bottle as I look around to make sure no one is watching me.

A sense of sadness purges my thoughts as I scan the large room. Everyone is having so much fun. There's laughter, dancing, kissing, and talking all around me. And what am I doing? I'm in a beautiful Oscar de la Renta gown, sabotaging my dragon wench nemesis. Something that seemed so fantastical just an hour ago suddenly seems so juvenile and ridiculous. Why can't I be focusing on fun like everyone else? Why have I devoted this whole year to Britney Taylor? First, by trying to impress her . . . and second, by getting even and trying to make her miserable.

I become shamefaced looking around at all my fellow classmates, having the best night of their lives, all the while knowing that *my* night has been planned purely around making Britney Taylor a mutant freak.

Glancing back at my three friends again, I suddenly wonder if they would even be my friends at all if it weren't for our common hatred of Britney and her Lipstick Laws.

Although perched over Britney's drink is not the best place or time to be rethinking the last year of my life, I can't help my conscience from not allowing me to go through with the peanut oil plan. Is this how I want to remember my sophomore spring formal? What if her allergy is worse than I think? What if people think I tried to kill her? What if Matt catches me? Why can't I just forget about our rivalry and have a good time? I can't let myself stoop to her level tonight.

"I'm better than this," I whisper to myself, screwing the cap back on the bottle. I know I'll be disappointing Mel, Ashley, and Rachel horribly, but I decide that if they really are my friends, they'll understand . . . and we'll be able to put this all aside, forget about the Lipstick Laws, and just have fun tonight.

I turn around with a burst of inner maturity and self-pride, finding myself a foot away from Mr. Hottie-Body Brentwood. His smile is contagious. Although, I notice that his face looks a little different . . . I can't quite put my finger on what's changed, however.

"April! You look great!" he says, appraising me from head to toe.

"Thanks!" I blush, shoving the small bottle hurriedly into my shiny silver clutch. "I—"

I don't get another syllable out before I hear an intrusive high-pitched voice behind me. "Well, well, well . . . I don't recognize you without the Brillo pad on your head."

I turn around to see a fuming Britney Taylor, arms crossed against her chest.

"Perfect timing, Bowers; you wait till I leave to try to steal my date. Get a clue; he doesn't want you."

"It's not what you think, Brit," I say, nicer than usual, hoping we can both act like grownups here.

"No?" she says crossly.

"We're . . . we're just friends," I babble, looking at Matt to back up my claim with a nod. "I have a date; I don't want yours."

"Right, some freak funnel, I heard," Erin says, standing next to Britney protectively.

I ignore Erin and look directly at Britney. "I don't want to fight anymore. This whole year has been wasted on us fighting. Wanna call a truce?"

She stares at me blankly. "Nope."

"I know you weren't always like this. You were a good person before the Lipstick Laws."

"What the hell are you talking about?" She blinks wildly.

"I know that you were hurt by your parents' divorce . . . and being called Donut. You only created the Lipstick Laws to protect yourself from being hurt again, didn't you?" I say, trying my best hand at psychotherapy.

A troubled expression falls on her face. Her eyes become glossy as she stares at me, frozen in thought. Is my impromptu speech actually working?

"You don't need to keep bringing the pain from your past into the present by hurting everyone around you." I strain a compassionate smile before glancing over at my friends across the room. They look panicked, most likely thinking that Britney has caught me trying to spike her drink.

She breaks her haunted gaze and snaps, "Are you trying to be a therapist, April? 'Cause therapists have to be smart. You must've missed that memo."

"No," I say. "I'm just trying to say that you don't have to be like this anymore. You don't have to follow the Lipstick Laws and hold your friends to these impossible standards. You can't be happy this way, Britney."

"They're not impossible standards for people who are worthy. And you aren't. You don't have what it takes to be one of us."

"Thank goodness," I mutter under my breath. "Listen, it doesn't have to be like this between us."

"If you're trying to make nice all of a sudden, I don't play that way." She glares at me.

"Look, we don't have to be friends. That's not what I'm trying to do here. In fact, we're probably better off not being friends."

Britney laughs exaggeratedly. "You got *that* right!"

"But," I say, feeling drained, "we can at least be civil."

She puts her hand on her hip and points at me assertively. "I'd rather drink poison than be civil with you."

For a moment I consider handing her the peanut oil bottle and suggesting that she chug it. Instead, I shrug my shoulders and say, "Hey, I tried."

I turn to Matt, who looks particularly bewildered by the situation.

"This is my cue to leave. Have a great night." I smile at him and turn to walk away.

Before I get too far, I hear Britney yell, "You may have gotten rid of your fugly frizzy hair, but there's nothing you can do to get the fugly out of your face."

I don't respond, which makes Britney even more annoyed. Her irritated tone is instantly heightened. "Why don't you look at me when I talk to you, freak funnel?"

I hear Matt and Jess plead with her to drop it and leave me alone. I feel like a spineless wimp, leaving the dirty work up to sympathetic observers. Feeling foolish, I turn around with my head held high and walk back to face her.

"Britney, c'mon, it's the spring formal! Let's just forget about us and have fun." I add, "On opposite sides of the room."

She screws her face up nastily and mimics me, " 'Let's just forget about us and have fun.' Yeah, right—like that's gonna happen!"

I roll my eyes, half regretting my choice to leave her drink alone.

"Real mature, Brit. Seriously, grow up and get a life." Then I look back at Matt, who looks even more embarrassed now, and say, "Hope you have fun with that mess."

As I'm walking away, I begin to notice the crowd parting around me. People are pointing behind me, and gasps are spreading like wildfire. Before I have time to turn around to see what the fuss is about, I feel a force of air swoosh against my back . . . followed by cold manicured hands groping the sides of my dress.

Before I know it, Britney Taylor has successfully captured and pulled out my chicken cutlet chestoid enhancers, presenting them unabashedly to the crowd of surprised onlookers like flopping fish made of flesh-colored Jell-O.

"Look, everyone! It's Boobless Bowers!" she shrieks in hysterics.

Before I've thoroughly processed what happened, I cover my sesame seed chest and drooping dress with my hands and hightail it to the ladies' room. I hear Britney's cackle and quiet gossiping fill the dance hall around me as I run in silent horror.

Tears flood my eyes and spill down my cheeks and onto my billowing dress below. My worst nightmare has come true. Worse yet, it all happened in front of Matt Brentwood. Now he and every other sophomore in the school know that I stuff my bra . . . and that I actually have boob buds the size of small paper cuts. I'm a loser . . . a boobicus minimus suffering, size 34C-obsessed, bosom-sculpting loser.

I run into the bathroom entrance, sobbing wildly. Not watching where I'm going, I bump into Darci Madison as she's walking out. Her enormous boobage stuffed into a corset-style dress is the last thing that I need to see right now.

"You okay?" she asks, concerned.

I can't process a normal response. I manage to whimper, "No boobs" like a loon before retreating into the last stall of the long bathroom.

Images of Britney Taylor prancing around the dance hall showing everyone my chicken cutlet fake boobs torment my mind as I lock myself into the cramped stall.

Am I out of my mind? Why did I think I could reason with her? She's completely unreasonable! Why didn't I just spike her drink? I was right there—the opportunity practically hit me in the face . . . and I didn't do it. I knew she was bound to do something like this to me . . . and I had the chance to sabotage her first . . . and I didn't take it! If I had just gone through with the plan, instead of dancing around with my chestoid enhancers, she'd be hobbling around like a mutant hived freak!

Panicking, I assess the damage done to my bra and top half of the dress now that my chest has been deflated like popped balloons. My bra cups are sagging dramatically without anything to hold them up. It's at this moment that I realize my new permanent address is this bathroom stall. I am never going to let myself leave it to face the scrutiny waiting for me outside this toileted fortress.

chapter twenty-three

After several minutes of crying and contemplating drowning myself in the toilet, I hear the clanking of dress shoes coming into the bathroom. God, please don't let this be Britney or anyone else ready to torture me some more. The long strides get closer and closer. I cover my mouth, holding back any noise, tears still streaming down my face.

"April?"

Phew . . . It's just Melanie. But I don't feel like talking.

"April, are you in here? I know you are," she says, her shoes clanking to my stall. She taps on the door and pleads, "Talk to me!"

"I want to be left alone," I say, adding, "*forever!*"

"What happened?" she asks. "I mean, I heard what happened . . . but is it true?"

"Yep," I moan, looking down at my drooping bra and dress top.

"But why: Did she catch you spiking her drink?"

"No! You wanna know why? Because I'm stupid! Stupid, stupid, stupid!" I vent. "I was right there! Her drink was right in front of me . . . and what did I do? I started feeling bad for plotting something like that! Can you believe it? Look where it got me! My boobs were dethroned in front of our whole school!"

"April, you're *not* stupid!" Melanie emphasizes. "You're *nice!*

Nice is a good thing! It takes a strong person to fight back spite. You should be proud of yourself. I am."

"Oh, yeah . . . real proud. Proud to be Boobless Bowers hiding out in a bathroom stall," I mumble sarcastically.

I know Mel is just trying to make me feel better, but she's not the one who just had her chest deflated in front of everyone. I don't need pep talks about how "nice" I am and what a "strong" person I am. I can't bear to talk about this any more without puking all over my new dwelling.

Sniffling, I say, "If it's okay with you, I want to be left alone with my flat chest for a little while. I need to think."

"Listen, I'll leave for a bit, but I'm coming back to check on you. I know you're embarrassed, but you have nothing to be embarrassed about."

"Right. Tell me that when it happens to you."

"Britney's the one who should be embarrassed! Who does that? That's sexual harassment. You could sue her!"

"Call my lawyer," I gurgle out.

She ignores my comment and continues, "Well, when you decide to come out, I'll help you adjust your dress. I'll come back in a few minutes."

I don't bother telling her that this stall is my permanent residence. I remain silent while she stands outside the bathroom door for another minute before walking out and leaving me alone.

Shortly thereafter, I'm not at all happy when Melanie returns with many more clanking shoes following her to "check on me."

"I'm still thinking!" I sniffle, annoyed that she didn't give me enough time to mourn my deceased boob buds.

"April, you okay?" Rachel asks.

"No—I'm humiliated!"

"C'mon, April. It's okay . . . most people didn't even see it," Ashley says.

"Matt Brentwood saw it!" I shout miserably.

"He's not God! Who cares what he thinks?" Ashley replies forcefully.

"Yeah . . . and he totally plucks his eyebrows," Rachel adds, knowing this is a huge turnoff of mine, probably assuming this revelation will make me feel better. It doesn't.

"Does not," I defend him.

Ashley calmly reiterates Rachel's claim. "No, April . . . he does. I can tell. Maybe he has a unibrow without hot wax. You never know these days."

Melanie decides to interject some logic. "So what if Matt saw? You make him out to be such a great guy, but he isn't. I mean, look—he's at the spring formal with Britney Taylor—a vile, airheaded brat! He knows you guys hate each other. He obviously doesn't care about your feelings."

"She asked him," I say quietly.

"And he could have said no. He hasn't even hardly talked to you since she asked him anyhow, has he? He's a jerk!" Melanie retorts.

I don't respond; my boobage has already been stripped away, and now my friends want to tamper with my idealistic image of Mr. Hottie-Body Brentwood.

Melanie persists, "Look, we didn't come in here to argue with you. We just came in here to show you something . . . something important . . . really important."

"What?" I say.

"You'll have to come out," Rachel says.

"If you guys snatched my boobs back from Brit-brat, it's not like I can just go ahead and stuff them back in after what happened."

"That's not it," Mel says. "What we want to show you will make you feel better. Promise."

After several minutes of pleading for me to emerge from the stall . . . and promising that they'll barricade the door to prevent anyone else from coming into the bathroom, I decide to open the door. Just for a second.

"Don't look at my chest." I cover it as I peep out the door. "What do you want?"

Melanie smiles. "You have to come out all the way first."

"Fine," I groan, continuing to guard my deflated chest and drooping dress. Immediately, I'm startled to see Mark Rhinehart next to the girls.

"What's he doing here?" I yell in dismay, turning around swiftly to return to my stall.

Melanie grabs me quickly and says, "Don't worry, April, he's harmless! Promise. Just give us ten minutes. That's all."

"Fine," I groan, more self-conscious now that a boy is in the ladies' room with us. "What do you want?"

They all smile, and Melanie moves to the sink. A bit irritated, I tap my shoe on the hard tile floor, waiting for this "important" something to happen.

"We just want to show you that you're not the only one hiding something you don't like about yourself," Melanie says as she opens her sparkling clutch to pull out a contact case.

She then takes out her contacts one by one and replaces them with a pair of glasses that were stowed safely in her clutch. I've never seen her in glasses before . . . and I get what she's trying to do . . . but wearing glasses is hardly the same as having your chestoid enhancers stolen in front of the school. Besides, Melanie still looks beautiful in a sophisticated, bookish way.

Like clockwork, Rachel takes over from there. "Do you ever wonder why I don't wear skirts, shorts, capris, or short dresses?" she asks me as she pulls her long black dress up to her calves. "I have cankles! Big, fat cankles! Look—my calves have eaten my ankles! I have four knees!"

She dances around goofily, showing her ankles. I can't help but give a little giggle. They're not as bad as she thinks, and they're definitely not as bad as being Boobless Bowers.

Ashley takes the lead after Rachel's ankle jig. "Mark, make sure no one comes in, 'kay?" Mark goes to the door like a security guard, and Ashley continues, "You may wish you had bigger curves, April, but be glad you don't have mine." She pulls up her dress, showing a body shaper underneath it. She pulls it off slowly like a snake shedding skin and holds it up for me to see. "Spanx—I don't go anywhere without them. Look, my dress doesn't even fit now that I'm not being sucked in. I have more rolls than a bakery." She points to her midsection, where her dress fabric is now tugging and creased.

Although it makes me feel great to have friends who are willing to point out their flaws on my behalf, I'm still humiliated about what happened to me. I look down, feeling guilty for not feeling better.

Before I have time to say anything foolish, Melanie says, "We saved the best part for last. Mark, it's your turn."

My attention is immediately drawn to Mark, who's walking back from guarding the bathroom entrance. I look at the girls skeptically; they giggle when he begins to speak.

"So . . . ah . . . I guess you know my secret . . . you know . . . ah . . . from the library . . ." he says, his face getting red.

I nod in acknowledgment, feeling unprepared for what's to come. He begins to unbutton his dress shirt. I shield my eyes as he takes it off, forgetting that my dress is drooping. I hear the girls whisper and laugh, and my curiosity cork pops. I take a peek and find Mark Rhinehart standing before me in a red lace bra and tuxedo pants.

"Oh my gosh!" I exclaim.

"I told you you're not the only one, April," Melanie states, trying to keep a straight face. "See, we all have secrets and imperfections. I bet everyone on that dance floor has something about themselves that they want to change or are trying to hide. Sure, most of our flaws weren't displayed in front of other people, but we're all prepared to go out like this—imperfections and all—and enjoy the formal with you."

"Well, all of us except for Mark," Ashley admits. "He'll get kicked out dancing in that getup."

Mark blushes while putting his white collared shirt back on. He then slips out of the bathroom, leaving me with the girls and the disturbingly humorous image of his chest cemented into my mind.

Melanie continues, "So don't let what Britney did ruin your night. She doesn't deserve to ruin your formal. You are beautiful—stacked bra or not!"

"And we love you!" Rachel adds, still hiking her dress up to show her ankles.

"Please come back out with us. We can put everything behind us and just have fun. Look, I'll even wear my Spanx over my head if it'll make you feel better!" Ashley says.

I don't know if I want to laugh or cry. I'm overwhelmed with emotion. I can't believe I was actually questioning whether these girls would be my friends if it weren't for our common loathing of Britney Taylor. They are true friends . . . and I'd choose true friends over a size 34C chest any day.

They look at me anxiously, hoping I'll concede to going back onto the dance floor with them. After what they've done for me, I'm not going to let them down.

I glance down at my hopeless chest and ask, "Can you help me fix my dress?"

"You bet!" Mel leaps toward me. She takes a bobby pin out from her updo and motions for me to turn around. While she's adjusting the loose crisscross straps and fabric to fit my flat chest more snugly, someone enters the bathroom in a rush.

We look up, startled to see Jessica standing at the entrance, smiling breathlessly.

Rachel snaps, "Get out of here, Jessica! Lipstick Lawlords are not welcome!"

"But . . . I'm not! I'm a Lipstick Lawbreaker now!" she responds earnestly, making her way closer to me and Melanie.

"What do you mean?" I scowl at her, feeling vulnerable and embarrassed again.

She holds up a silver thumbtack from one of the spring formal banners and smiles. "Let's just say Brit-brat Taylor isn't as curvy anymore, either. Go have a look."

Jessica points to the exit. Confused and intrigued, we all peer out from the bathroom at the chaotic scene on the dance floor. Britney is having a temper tantrum center stage. The front of her dress is streaming with water and she's grasping the top of it up while screaming like a psycho. Erin and Brianna are swarming around her frantically . . . only to be met by curse words flying from Britney's mouth. As far as I can see, Matt Brentwood is nowhere in sight. I don't blame him; it seems like Britney's head is about to spin in circles.

"What happened?" the girls and I exclaim simultaneously.

Jessica smiles. "I popped her water bra."

"You didn't!" we say admiringly.

"I did!" Jess singsongs proudly, displaying the shiny thumb-tack again.

"Brit's cleavage is fake?" I say, totally flabbergasted by this revelation.

"Yep. She's worn a water bra since seventh grade," Jess explains.

I shake my head, thinking this can't be true. "But, I saw her in a bikini . . . and she looked perfect!"

Jessica laughs. "Her mom bought her water gel inserts to go in her bikini tops. Oops—looks like her big secret has suddenly leaked!"

I can't help but smile at the irony of this moment. Little did I know, Britney and I had more in common than I ever thought. All along, I've been putting her on this beauty pedestal . . . thinking her body is completely flawless . . . jealous of her cleavage . . . wishing I had a chest like hers. Meanwhile, I've been envious of a water bra this whole time. Britney's a bosom sculptor just like me!

"I guess what goes around comes around! Karma just bit 'er in the butt . . . I mean, boobs," I say, before bursting into uproarious laughter with the rest of the girls.

chapter twenty-four

Feeling a heightened sense of euphoria once Britney and her followers leave the formal in a frenzy, I decide that it's time to celebrate with my friends, including our newest member of the Lipstick Lawbreakers.

We're dancing, laughing, and having a better time than I expected until someone taps my shoulder. I can recognize his cologne from anywhere. Abercrombie Fierce is a scent that sends me into ecstasy. However, the whole "Boobless Bowers" incident is still fresh in my mind, and I turn around with angst as I—adorned with my newly flattened chest—face Mr. Hottie-Body Brentwood.

"Can I talk to you for a second?" he asks over the DJ's music.

"Sure."

We walk to the closest wall to get some privacy. I cross my arms over my chest to hinder his view of the damage.

"I've been wanting to talk to you all night. You look gorgeous," he says with a smile.

What? He still thinks I look gorgeous after everything that went down? Does he not care that I'm flat as a chalkboard?

"Thanks," I say. "I've felt better."

"I'm sorry, April; you were right about her," he says expressively. "She shouldn't have done that to you."

I feel my face getting red just thinking about it. "Yeah, well, it wasn't a bucket of fun. It's not your fault, though. Honestly, I just want to forget about it."

"Ditto. I just want to forget about her. I feel like I haven't been myself since she asked me to this formal. She's been so obsessed with changing me, I don't even think she knows who I am."

"What do you mean?" I ask, relieved to depart from the Boobless Bowers topic.

"That girl has been trying to tell me what I can and can't do for the last month. She's a controlling nutcase."

"Yep, that's Britney," I say sympathetically. "She's crazy."

"She even got me to wax my eyebrows! *Wax my eyebrows!* Can you believe it? I don't even know how she talked me into it."

That's what looks different! My friends were right! I look at his freshly waxed eyebrows and shudder. She probably did that because she knows it's my pet peeve.

"I wouldn't make that a habit," I say.

"I don't plan on it. I'm staying away from hot wax and Britney from now on."

"You'll be much better off," I say. "She tries to change everyone around her to fit her crazy standards. She wants robots, not friends. It's pathetic."

Out of the corner of my eye, I catch a glimpse of Delvin McGerk sitting by himself, looking bored to pieces. He sees me and waves graciously. Then, like a racing comet, it hits me—oh my gosh, I've been just like Britney Taylor! I've used Delvin for selfish purposes just like Britney used Matt. I've tried to change and control everything about him just like Britney does to everyone. I've completely dismissed his feelings to make myself look and feel better. How can I be so stupid? How could I be so Brat-ney Taylorish? Guilt overwhelms me immediately.

I'm reeling with disgust for myself when I hear Matt asking me to dance to the slow song that's just come on. "So, what d'ya say? Wanna dance?"

The timing couldn't be worse. I want to feel him holding me, but I just can't dance with him knowing that Delvin is miserable in a corner because of me—especially after all he's done for me. I walked into this formal too much like Britney Taylor . . . and I want to leave as April Bowers.

I may kick myself for this later, but with a newfound will-power that I would have never had an hour ago, I say, "I'd really love to, Matt, but I already have a date. I'm sorry. I should dance with him."

And then, without a second thought, I leave Matthew Brentwood wanting more. I've been chasing Mr. Hottie-Body all year. It's about time for him to start chasing me. A girl has to play hard to get sometimes. After all, guys like a chal-lenge, right?

As I approach Delvin, I feel all the negativity that's sur-rounded me this last year melt away. A rush of positive energy paints a smile on my face.

"Come here often?" I say to him with a cheesy grin.

"I-I thought you ditched me. I thought for sure I'd be driv-ing home alone," he says.

Teasing playfully, I say, "Well, let's see, if you're a good dancer, maybe I'll let you escort me back home in your *new* Camaro."

He jumps to his feet. "Are you asking me to dance, April Bow—" He covers his mouth instantly and looks at me like he's ruined his chances. "Sorry, I know I'm not supposed to say your full name in informal conversations."

"Don't worry about it, McGerk. It's kind of catchy. I don't mind anymore. April Bowers it is. Now let's do this thing before we miss the song," I say, pulling him to the middle of the dance floor.

It turns out Delvin's a decent dancer . . . and he's actually pretty funny when I'm not trying to pick him apart. The formal turns out to be a blast. I don't think about Britney Taylor or the Lipstick Laws for the rest of the night. I'm surrounded by people who love me—true friends . . . and yes, now that I've put Delvin through the wringer and he still talks to me, I consider him a friend, too.

It's crazy, but I'm not even sure that anyone (other than the witnesses of the Boobless Bowers incident) noticed my new flat look. I think I was making my sesame seed chest into a way bigger issue than it ever should have been. The people who matter don't care what size bra I wear . . . and the people who do care . . . well, I guess they don't matter. I wasted way too many tissues over the last couple years being a 34C-obsessed bosom sculptor—and I think that now it's more important to focus on being me.

When Delvin pulls into my driveway at the end of the night, I'm positive that the whole neighborhood has been awakened by the screeching of his brakes.

He puts the car in park, and I grab his digital camera.

"How 'bout a picture to end the night?" I suggest.

"Really?" He smiles.

"Yeah, say cheese!" I say, putting my head next to his, smiling for the flash.

We take a few more pictures before I decide that it's time to go inside. I reach for the door handle.

"No, no . . . wait. I wouldn't be any gentleman at all if I let you get out on your own. Stay right there," Delvin says. He scurries out the driver's side and around the car to open my door for me.

"Thanks," I say, accepting his hand to help me out.

He walks me up to the door, and we stand in awkward silence for a few seconds.

"I had a lot of fun tonight, Delvin."

"Me too," he says, inching closer.

I know he wants a kiss . . . and no, I'm not going to *make out* with Delvin McGerk . . . but I *do* decide to kiss him on the cheek. His eyes stay closed for a moment after my peck. His face lights up, and we both smile clumsily.

"Well," he says, "I guess I should let you get inside for the night. Thanks for being a great date."

"No—thank *you!*" I say genuinely.

And then, after a goodbye hug, I walk into my house, where I'm met by a beeping cell phone. A text message from Matt appears:

> Can I get a rain check
> 4 that dance?
> I'd LOVE 2 see U
> tomorrow!

Smiling to myself, I realize that it's definitely better to be wanted than to be the one wanting. And with that, I go to bed a proud Lipstick Lawbreaker and an ex-bra-stuffer.

ACKNOWLEDGMENTS

Writing isn't always a solitary feat, especially when there's a group of encouraging people cheering you on. It's a delight to be able to extend special thanks to those who have helped me the most:

Mom and Dad, your unwavering support and faith in my aspirations and talents make me believe that my hard-to-reach goals are reachable. You've given me unconditional love from day one, and for this, I am lucky and forever grateful.

Todd, thank you for helping me on my road to publication. I am eternally thankful for all you've done, and for the many laughs you've provided me through the years.

Kim, your positivity is infectious and your pep talks are unparalleled. Thank you for never letting me doubt myself.

Mike, you've believed in me and my dreams since we met. I will always remember and appreciate your encouragement.

To the many family members, friends, special teachers, and fellow writers who remain nameless here, I will always be thankful for your positive presence in my life.

I also want to send a huge thank you to the wonderful people at Houghton Mifflin Harcourt for acquiring and guiding my manuscript to publication. This is especially relevant to my amazing editor, Julia Richardson. Your guidance and enthusiasm have made the publishing process both enlightening and enjoyable.

Finally, I'd like to thank *you* (the reader) for choosing to read this book.

I hope you enjoy it and I'd love to hear from you!
www.amyholder.com